"Begin at the beginning," my Michael said tersely. "Don't do a Star Wars."
So here I am at the beginning. No flinching.

FOREIGN

147 DAYS   VOLUME 1

ACT 1
MODERN SAVAGES

Written and Illustrated

by

Alitha E. Martinez

CONTENTS

· SINE METU AD ASTRA ·

ЧУЖА

F·O·R·E·I·G·N

Written and Illustrated
by
Alitha E. Martinez

F·O·R·E·I·G·N

Ariotstorm Productions LLC.

First softcover edition: May 2015

Martinez, Alitha Evelyn
Foreign: 147 Days, Damnatio Memorae: a novel / by Alitha E. Martinez – 1st ed.

ISBN
978-0-9903188-4-2
0990318842

Summary
Through the Unity Program, the United Earth Defense Force (UEDF) try
to reconnect with their home planet, Earth. But the world has changed
in ways that make the space nomads of the Nation Fleet too foreign
to fit back into Earth's complex society.

Printed in the United States of America

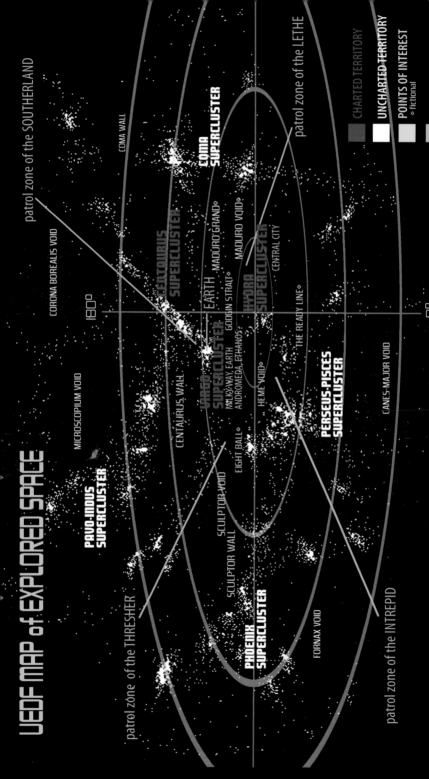

UEDF MAP of EXPLORED SPACE

patrol zone of the SOUTHERLAND

CORONA BOREALIS VOID

COMA WALL

180°

MICROSCOPIUM VOID

CENTAURUS SUPERCLUSTER

COMA SUPERCLUSTER

MADURO GRAND°

EARTH

MADURO VQID°

GODGIN STRAIT°

VIRGO SUPERCLUSTER

CENTRAL CITY

HYDRA SUPERCLUSTER

CENTAURUS WALL

MILKY-WAY EARTH
ANDROMEDA, ETHANOS

patrol zone of the LETHE

PAVO-INDUS SUPERCLUSTER

HEME VOID°

0°

"THE READY LINE"

EIGHT BALL°

SCULPTOR VOID

PERSEUS-PISCES SUPERCLUSTER

CANES-MAJOR VOID

patrol zone of the THRESHER

SCULPTOR WALL

PHOENIX SUPERCLUSTER

FORNAX VOID

patrol zone of INTREPID

CHARTED TERRITORY

UNCHARTED TERRITORY

POINTS OF INTEREST
° fictional

POINT ADMIRAL LOCATIONS

"Toesa, toesa, what are we going to do?"

Act 1
Modern Savages

Chapter 1 ─────────────────────

Afternoon.
Godgin Strait.

"Toesa, what shall we do?" Signe pleaded like a helpless child to Isolda, using the honorific title of *toesa*—my sister who leads me. She was already setting up her defense.

"Be quiet!" Blobs of sweat rolled through Isolda's pixie-cropped brown hair and splattered on the backs of her wiry hands. It cut her breath to see her own fingers gnarled like hairless paws, and trembling so badly that she could hardly get them to work. Perhaps it was providence that the UEDF's TAU Sword, and its compliment of Valfore star jets drifting past the window, could provide her with the proper motivation to unbuckle her subordinate and pull her to her feet. "Move quickly!" She speared through the thickening crowd with purpose.

"What are we going to do?" Signe repeated while she jostled to and fro in Isolda's narrow wake.

"Just hurry and don't panic." Futile words, a measly utterance over a scene of bedlam. They didn't soothe Isolda's own pounding heart as she began to wonder if she'd have to face punishment alone, or if the mousy little wisp she was forced to align herself with would accept her share of the blame.

In a moment like this there were a lot of *if onlys* that played on the mind. If only their race hadn't been driven to near-extinction by one careless act. If only the few surviving refugees had chosen to stay on their home world instead of taking up a nomadic life in space—which they were neither prepared for, nor did they know anything about. If only she could have remained a carefree girl running up and down the breezy hills of Ethanos. She would have taken a male by now. There would have been children at her hearth, and she would have only known the useless blonde by her side in passing in the village square. If only, if only....

"To all passengers," the Muu captain's wobbly voice broke across their backs like a cold wave. She was noticeably anxious as she recited the UEDF's warning verbatim. "Acting under the Article of No Quarter, the UEDF has the right to search any Muu vessel for time-sensitive targets. Cooperation is mandatory."

Voices rose in a chorus of dread. There was no hiding the alarm of suddenly falling under the UEDF's scrutiny. If the biggest, baddest standing army in the known universe found cause to put its eye on such an insignificant bug drifting through space, it certainly wasn't to pass out gift baskets.

"Return to your assigned seat."

Which was impossible to do.

"And present your boarding pass and identification to the UEDF officers."

Which no sane person would do willingly.

"They are going to search every inch of this ship," Signe squeaked out the inexorable truth. "Perchance with scans and frightful probes."

"For goods stolen from them by raiders. Nothing more." Isolda took the announcement like a death sentence in spite of the optimistic words that came out of her mouth.

"But we stole from them, too."

"Not goods, and that is all they are looking for!" She felt the need to qualify their position. After all, they weren't greedy thieves looking to fill their pockets with more of what they already had kindred to the panicked fools spinning around them like moths. "We are scientists. We will show them our manifest and say that our cargo is too sensitive to search—"

"AGH! We are all dust in space! The *Youee* will blow us to dust in space!" A man sprung out of the grip of reality, vomiting a disastrous premonition that was hard to disregard as far-fetched. Isolda would have stopped to give him the sobering slap he needed if she had a moment to spare.

The dingy Muu transport wasn't built for comfort. It was all jump seats and cavernous holds mishmashed together on two of the most narrow, impassable decks either of the women had seen in all of their wanderings. The rusty stairs rattled under the weight of the stampeding herd as they tried to descend onto the cargo deck in a burbling conglomerate. The old barge listed sharply when the TAU Sword's umbilical attached to the aft air lock. Isolda stumbled five full steps and caught herself against the wall only to be bowled down the rest of the flight by Signe's uncontrolled fall.

"By all our craven gods, girl-ean, can you not help yourself!" Isolda despaired in their native language as she hauled them both to their feet with a sharp stitch of pain hobbling her every step. She was tired of having to keep them gainfully motivated all by herself. She couldn't understand why such a devious woman wasn't equally as ambitious. "The crew will try to stall for time but eventually the UEDF will board. We must keep going."

"But to what end, toesa?" Signe mewled as they pushed past fat, well-robed merchants frantically checking their inventory for anything that could be confiscated.

"Where did this come from? Fringe? That is a port that the *Youee* uses. Was it stolen?" one frantic voice questioned.

"We paid fair market value in good coin, sir. How can the *Youee* take it?"

"Because it is stolen!"

Frayed nerves sparked heated arguments in every corner of the great hold. Isolda tripped the door lock once they'd passed through to the private compartment area. That would buy them a minute's peace and, hopefully, another to work with.

"We have to be quick!" she instructed as they turned into their small rented stow.

The eight-by-ten space was bathed in red emergency lights that washed out the wall-mounted display screens and exit signs. Isolde never understood the use of the color of blood as a warning. It just seemed like overkill. Wasn't reality stark enough without glutting it with an intrinsic sheen of terror?

Their three crates were too big to empty out, or summarily destroy in a way that would absolve them;

most especially the gargantuan rectangular box that took up nearly the entire length of the room. It sat there like a spotlit curiosity that she knew no agent would be able to resist.

Isolda unpacked the crowbars, but Signe stood frozen in a stupor born of all of the things she inherently lacked, like the ability to plan on her feet and a reliable spine. "What will we do?"

"Help me!" Isolda pried open the lid of the rectangular box, exasperated to the brink of weeping if she still had her complete tear ducts.

A crate made of wood should have had no mechanisms to hiss or vent the way this oversized box did once its lid had been breached. A computerized warning sounded, *"Stasis field interrupted,"* and the truth of it was revealed to be a very sophisticated, streamlined, medical stasis tube complete with its own power source.

At first glance, the women were a pitiful amalgam of unfortunate genetics, meanly packaged in the tiniest, most useless, bodies that any make of warrior could come in. Isolda skinny and dark, with not much beauty to speak of. And her polar opposite in Signe, barely more shapely, pink and twee, if not for the make up she slathered on her baby-cute face. Still, they were Kitteren demi-warriors. Hoisting the unconscious naked man out of the disguised stasis tube wouldn't have been a great feat for either of them alone, much less working together.

"The shallow sleep never took full effect." Signe noticed that his skin was degrees warmer and more supple than it should have been.

"Right now that works in our favor." Isolda surprised herself with the depths of her newfound ability to speak the good of a circumstance. She opened the bag she had packed with clothes for the specimen. Never once in all her careful plotting did she imagine that she'd be dressing her subject in haste on the cold rusted deck of a ship with the UEDF bearing down on her head. She nearly laughed out loud wondering which star would burn out if she were allowed to succeed at one thing in this life.

"Ogh!" Signe complained as she bullied the crisp fabric up his slippery arm. "We will never be able to dress him properly in time."

"Anything above naked will do."

"But a male would sooner be laid bare than be seen draped improperly in public. The part of his legs alone is a pity enough to draw unwanted attention—"

"Oh for the love of fair gods, Signe, these are modern times! The UEDF are about to show you such ferocious things wrapped in male's skin, the likes of which only our trod-down ancestors could attest to, yet you feel spared enough to worry about the set of one cretin's kuffiya? Off we go!"

"Uhnnn…where?" The man began to come to as they bumbled down the hall toward the forward elevator banks. There were enough half-faint, sweat-soaked people hanging onto one other to make their little gang seem commonplace.

"Thirty-three life forms detected in forward cargo bay." The announcement of a remote probe's discovery set off a fresh panic, but Isolda had come too far and done too much to be stopped short now. She hewed a path to the slowly closing doors and jammed both Signe and the groggy man into the elevator ahead of her reedy frame.

The passenger deck was awash with chaos. The petrified women weren't the only ones with incriminating secrets. People rushed to and fro creating just the right amount of camouflage for an enterprising few who knew that, for all of the calamity and awe they were capable of under other circumstances, the UEDF Tactical Armored Unit's officers had no authority to fire on non-aggressive civilians. All they could do was stand aside, huge phallic guns pointed at the ceiling, and let them flee, which would work just fine for the plan Isolda had come up with. She steered their little party into the deserted passenger cabin, right to the middle row, out in plain view.

"Leave him here." She dumped the man into a seat.

"Ohhhh…where am I?" he groaned with burgeoning clarity.

"But our investment will be lost." Signe huffed at the pitiful waste. She wasn't alone in her lamentations. Isolda paused: months of extensive research, covert maneuvering, round-the-clock surveillance, and firing up the courage to follow through with the most daring scheme anyone was fool enough to conceive of—let alone actuate—was about to be left flopped down abandoned when they were so close to achieving their goal that she could practically smell the sweet air of their new homeworld.

"The crux unbound!" Isolda pulled her bumbling confederate along to join the mob. She watched Signe's bottom lip swell a full inch off of her face in a silly pout and marveled at how the greedy could always find time for greed.

Far forward there were tiers of escape pods being put to good use. Isolda decided to do the same with her demi-warrior strength and threw a shivering couple bodily out of the next pod set to depart.

Her words were as done as her deeds. In that cleansing silence she strapped herself into the three-point harness and left Signe to do the same without instruction or go bouncing off of the bulkheads when the pod launched automatically. The tiny craft had independent navigation.

It only took Isolda a minute to familiarize herself with the controls.

"Toesa, we are away." Signe heaved a great sigh of relief as the surrounded Muu transport grew small in the rear hatch.

"Yes, sister," Isolda agreed, finally able to exhale. She set the autopilot for the nearest planet. "Our accursed ancestors want to be avenged."

Captain Whip watched the escape pods scatter into the black from the stillness of *Kingdom Come's* cockpit. The Article of No Quarter was very specific, and rather favorable to the thieves; but they didn't seem to know it by the way they ran.

His twin brother's identical Valfore pulled slightly ahead of his in position. *Glory Hallelujah's* vanes retracted. Her auxiliary flaps lengthened and locked into alignment with her maneuvering and high-lift flaps. Her slate-grey wings swept back against their fixed gloves as if she were getting set to run. She looked like she was about to live up to their squadron name and start administering some *last rites* punctuated with a bullet, which was probably making a lot of very scared people soil their good clothes as they puttered along helplessly in minimally shielded life capsules.

"Hey, Wether, what're you up to?" Whip tittered.

"Just taxin' an' tormentin'," Wether confirmed his suspicions. *Glory Hallelujah's* echo location sent a ripple across the deep that lit up the position of each and every one of the transport's errant pods on their instrument panels.

Whip kept a visual on the TAU Sword's umbilical. If there was a vulnerable point in their offense it would be the delicate connection between the two ships. The desperate sort could seize a temporary—albeit ill-fated— advantage with a bit of sabotage.

"Lord Vahe sure loves to take his time." He whistled.

"Hush up now!" Wether snapped jokingly. "You want him ta hear you? Remember, we ain't but two hundred and twenty pounds sop wet. Even together we wouldn't be half of a challenge on our best day and his worst."

"Hee, hee, yeah."

Inside the Muu transport, with an uneasy calm being enforced by his small squadron, Lord Vahe chose to ignore the COM chatter. He'd had his fill of the mischievous and the wild.

He roamed away from the guard he stationed at the throughway to the Sword, reviewing the remote probe's sweep one last time, before moving into the aft entrance of the passenger cabin. He imagined that the Valfore pilots wouldn't be in such a playful mood if they were the ones trying to maneuver a three hundred pound armored battle suit through the constricted bowels of a rickety over-used storage bin.

On top of the tight fit, the integrity of the old deck plates were in serious question. Every footfall left impressions in its thin face. Lord Vahe had mapped the vessel's skeleton, and cautioned his men not to bunch up, and to walk along the support beams as much as they could before he let them take a single step out of the Sword's sure umbilical. Yet still, he expected to find himself in a free fall through to the lower deck at any given moment. His master-at-arms suggested the use of their Personnel Body Armor. Certainly the no-mecha gear would have been worlds easier to negotiate and just as intimidating on all of their no less than six-foot-seven, three hundred fifty pound bodies, but they wouldn't be nearly as protected.

No Quarter calls were rare, but always memorable in some unanticipated way. On the last one, the ship they boarded had been hastily boobytrapped just for them. As soon as they entered the cargo hold, a daisy-chained link of grit grenades seeded along the hull timed out and half of his detachment was blown into space. They were lucky to have survived the rending explosion and the vacuum considering how damaged the PBAs were; and there wasn't a single uncracked helmet among those who had escaped the ejection but not the blast radius. It was a costly debacle that made Lord Vahe even more judicious and completely untrusting of people who quailed en masse. There were wolves hidden among them, the very same ones who had been bold enough to steal from the *Youee* in the first place. They only feared the UEDF up close. If given half a chance they wouldn't hesitate to strike.

"What end, what now?" Vahe grunted, mid-slinging of his M256 assault rifle. His second-in-command, Commander Enver, was escorting the Muu captain to him for an audience. The woman had a harrowed look about her, as if she were going to the gallows unsung.

"Please, my lord." She knew who he was by the sight of his onyx black armor alone, and how to address him so as not to supplementarily incur his wrath. "When can we be on our way?"

"Just as soon as we offload our stolen goods," he answered her without prevarication.

"I would not know yours from whose. There were three hundred-sixty passengers on board, each with their own cargo. My only occupation was to ferry them safely to Godgin II." Her words sputtered and dipped.

All of his intra-helmet display panels lit up before his eyes with reports of the chemical changes in her body. Elevated heart rate, increased serum calcium and neutrophilic leukocytes. Constriction of the peripheral blood vessels, piloerection and dyspepsia inducing flatulence. He didn't need bloated scientific terminology when he could see the fear dancing in her eyes. She was in a roll-around fight with her every self-preserving impulse to continue speaking calmly while staring up at the ghostly Rorschach image savagely painted on his faceplate.

"I suggest you go scoop up your peas. There are at least fifty escape pods bobbing in space nearby and thrice that many making good time across the far away. Leave us to finish without further ado." Of all the things indicated, lying wasn't one of them. He intended to flip her out of the hot seat as quickly as possible.

"Yes, my lord." She bowed respectfully as she beat a hasty retreat.

"Sir." Master Sergeant Yehu radioed in. "We have located our supplies."

"I am on my way down," he responded as he started toward the forward elevators with his soldiers trailing closely behind. No one took notice of the lone passenger still in his seat.

"W-wait...Lord Vahe...please...." The man clamped an iron grip on the last TAU officer in line.

"Sir, we are not here for you." Commander Enver carefully unfolded the man's damp hand from his gun belt.

"Ad...miral Vahe!!" the sickly man screamed with strength he couldn't spare.

Lord Vahe turned, a little weary of having to placate the overwrought one by one, but willing enough to give such a last-ditch effort the attention it deserved. Besides, precious few—even within the UEDF—called him by his rank, and he was curious to learn what made this stranger-out of-nowhere so bold.

"Sir…UEDF…Captain Aaron Hjorth…squadron Crazy Eights…I'm…." The pleading face was slick with anxious tears. He fought his own frailty to speak, but his consciousness gave out before he could finish.

"Captain?" Commander Enver alarmed at the prospect of this supposed stranger being one of their own.

"Confirm his identity." Lord Vahe opened the man's collar as his second administered the stick test. He didn't need a DNA field screening to tell him what his old friend's tattoos could. In the entire universe, the citizenry of the Nation Fleet were the only ones who wore markers on their flesh as a personal choice. Captain Hjorth was very proud of his full suit. It took the artists of the Hori Guild years to complete the masterwork of ancient mystical creatures locked in combat and beautiful renderings of floral geneses that hadn't bloomed on any planet in a thousand years. He'd show off his art with a lack of restraint that neither suited his age—or his station—but such was the human spirit. Its boldness galvanized three galaxies and kept them all banded strongly together.

An angry heat rose out of Lord Vahe's heart when his eyes met the familiar ink. Captain Hjorth was a friend. This pale recreation with the slimy, clammy skin was the leftovers someone forgot to take home. His biology had been altered away from its original design. This form of desecration wasn't common, but it was easy to recognize. Captain Aaron Hjorth, leader of the UEDF fighter squadron Crazy Eights, had been scrambled.

"Identification confirmed." Commander Enver read the results, fighting his own memories of the affable captain to maintain his professional objectivity. "How is this possible?"

"Captain Whip, an unexpected development," Lord Vahe reported. "We have come upon Captain Hjorth. ID confirmed."

"Aaron?" Whip bolted up straight with the shock. "What the fuck is he doin' on a Muu transport? Wether, can you get an update on the status of Crazy Eights Squad?"

"Already on it," Wether said.

Through their melded bond Whip could hear his brother's thoughts and the response from the Southerland's communication's tower that Wether reviewed in his mind before he made a mission-wide announcement.

Wether's voice was measured and low. "Basilisk confirmed the Eights checked in on time ten light-hours ago. Their next check isn't due for another sixteen shots. I told 'em to give them a shout."

Everyone already knew that it was a pointless exercise in protocol. Just rules to follow and to trip over to keep them neatly in line. But loyalty, duty—the life's blood of a soldier—could never be run dry by policy. Certain things would always be elementary. If their captain was here, half a galaxy away, abused, debilitated, and left in ruin, then the rest of the Eights had met with a worse fate.

Afternoon.
Earth.
Foundation Hill Men's Hospital.

"Ahh, kind Healers, one moment if you would!" Dr. Sunduvall's singsong timbre echoed through the main marble floor.

Vladimir and Tendart paused in their steps. It was most unusual for such a conservative warrior to raise her voice, let alone run to catch them before they could exit the building, since they had just left a consultation meeting with the team she was on.

"Good Doctor, have you forgotten something?" Vladimir asked once she had closed enough of the distance between them. He felt at liberty to speak since she had technically addressed them first, though he did pull his kuffiya up high to cover his head for the sake of propriety.

"Oh no…" she sputtered as she tried to catch her breath, "…I thought…that is…."

The Micromales faced her with their curiosity. Not only was she acting out of character, she was stumbling over her own thoughts, unable to find the words to express whatever it was that had her so frantic.

"Well…?" she hemmed. "Is it true that the Hand goes wherever you are needed?"

"Indeed we do," Vladimir responded, his interest boiling to a pitch.

"Have you employment for us?" Tendart cut to the chase. Unlike his close other, he wasn't fond of riddles. They had a full day's worth of caseloads to transcribe, which would take long enough without the delay of a protracted conversation.

"Since it is so, I do have need of your services…at least I fear that I do." She grew more shy with each word until they could hardly hear what she managed to drizzle out in the end.

Scandal was on the tip of her tongue. Sunduvall was a mindful family woman—long willed and deeply rooted in the community—but it seemed that even the most stalwart warrior was no better then she should be.

the community—but it seemed that even the most stalwart warrior was no better then she should be.

"I assure you, madam, we are the soul of discretion. Whate'er need you have, we will endeavor to serve you utterly." Tendart hoped that was the last assurance he'd have to offer her.

"I fear this enterprise." She strengthened enough to finally come clean. "It is too strange a thing, but I cannot feign ignorance o'er the matter. 'Tis on my father's account that I have come to you. It is likely that he breeds."

"Oh?" Vladimir found her concern quite puzzling. What could possibly be unusual about that?

"I have seen the signs of it, yea my father is a Human."

"Well…e'en so, Human males can be caught by the loins." Vladimir shrugged a little. "We are not strangers to delivering such men—"

"But a man such as my father?" She cut him short as she dared that one step closer than a warrior should to two lone men in public. "His age is advanced," she whispered huskily, "sixty-five years are on him."

The men finally understood. They came within a yard to keep as much of her confidence as decorum would allow.

"Y-you say?" Tendart's brow tightened into something just outside of a judgmental frown.

"Aye. Just so." Sunduvall nodded firmly. "When would it be possible for you to see him?"

"Forthwith!"

Chapter 2 ─────────────────────

Evening.
Earth.
Solito Lake Retirement Village.

Rows of quaint bungalows lined neatly landscaped cul-de-sacs. Everything was lush and green. Flowers bloomed, and trees stood tall in the crisp spring evening air as if this were the one spot on Earth where nature had forgiven man for the mortal wounds he had inflicted upon her.

Elderly Humans mulled about doing the most mundane tasks either of the Micromales had ever seen. Outside of this haven artificial lawns didn't need to be watered. Perpetual hedges never needed to be trimmed, and no one cooked in outdoor firepits, let alone the precarious-looking pots on stilts that were still smoldering in the open field beside a sprawling split-level log cabin. There was an engraved sign nestled in a pleasant arrangement of flowering bushes and well-placed stones that read *Clubhouse* in two languages that they recognized and three others that looked like neatly scribbled vandalism.

Funny little carts that didn't seem street worthy zipped along, peopled by the pair. Most curious of all, a young woman, walking an impossibly small dog—akin to a rat, with the same sort of slick fur and unsightly whip of a tail—hugged suggestively on the arm of a man whose cloth had rotted beyond all practical use. The public show of affection only served to embarrass what was left of him. Vladimir and Tendart had never seen the like, and they were silently concerned that Sunduvall was driving them into the heart of an inescapable wonderland.

Everyday life was a struggle on the poisoned Earth. Hardly anyone got along; and, when they did, it was only because one side had conceded defeat. It was strange to see such an easy blending of species, particularly where the Humans were concerned. There weren't many of them left on the planet, but they were a desperate, avaricious lot bent on having the run of things. But here, in this strange haven, there were no radical street preachers shouting their bitter predictions of genome extinction; no picketing protesters marching in endless circles; or shell-shocked citizens just trying to survive the day. People whose cloth had rotted—the elderly, as they were called by the Humans alone—could wear their years proudly without the fear of being mistaken for a plague beast and struck down. As doctors the Micromales knew that Humans could grow old, but so few got the chance that it was rare to come across anyone over the age of fifty. These people looked healthy and content. The more the Micromales saw the harder it was to believe that anyone in this place could be subject to the type of scandalous secret that Sunduvall had confessed.

"Is this some manner of exclusive territory?" Tendart had to ask just to be sure.

"No. My father moved to Earth three Human Years ago along with his compatriots from The United Earth Defense Force. In fact most of the residents are UEDF, with Keyvu and Kazen being the predominant languages. I think my father will speak Of Megt or Of Yomin depending on his mood. But it is late, so he might only manage Pan Minor or Of the Core. I suppose we shall see. Either way, he will not require a translator, unless you try to speak the Human's English." Sunduvall rambled from point to point as if she were speaking to herself. "Stand warned, my father is the most daring of his lot, yea, they are all rowdy. He and the rest of the Horde are fighter pilots very used to having their own rule and way. I have taken many disciplinary calls from the attending staff."

"To be sure." Tendart tried to pick the sense out of her many strange statements. She seemed to be relaying the antics of a petulant child instead of a grown man who should know better. He wondered if that was parcel to how Humans gained their age.

The opulent stretch of the clubhouse's lawn sloped gently to the banks of a narrow sparkling lake. The water's placid surface glistened like flecks of gold in the waning light. It ran nearly the entire length along the right side of the main road, meaning to thrill the eye with its manicured beauty. Sunduvall swung a left and pulled into the driveway of the third house on the half-circle street. Her grey luxury sedan dwarfed the compact city-car she'd parked behind.

Words began to flicker at the edge of Tendart's mind. At first they were unclear, like a muddled din echoing through a closed door. He reached to listen. The curiosity helped him to adjust the frequency until he was completely and comfortably attuned. He'd spent nearly all the years of his life in Vladimir's constant company. In many ways he was closer to him than he was to his brother by blood. Never was he more keenly aware of that fact than when he shared Vladimir's consciousness.

It wasn't by accident that they so often thought the same thoughts; or reacted like a verenigd to stimulation, as if they were one person in two bodies. He was hardly ever only himself when he was with Vladimir. Always a collection of them—a *we* above the I—though he wasn't any bit Yomin, more like an honorary member through their friendship.

Vladimir was so accustomed to having him in his matrix that he never begged pardon when he threw the door open, or stopped to wonder if it was a good time to be in thought. Tendart climbed out of the back seat of the car already deeply engrossed in Vladimir's mental commentary. Being avid auto enthusiasts, they were unified in the decision to use the moment it took for Dr. Sunduvall to gather her belongings to once-over the souped-up little city car with its Magnaflow dual-tipped exhaust valves giving away its specialized nature. They wondered if the high-sheen, ash blue paint job was a single nitrocellulose lacquer kit; or a two-stage urethane base coat with a clear-coat finish, which they were about to have a brief discussion over when they became keenly aware of being utterly, and suddenly, alone.

The streets were empty after the village square. Houses stood lonesome and dark. The Micromales considered that the people who worked were not yet at home. By this time of day in the Allied Defense Force base suburbs where they lived, families were sitting down to supper. Even in homes where the hour was kept it was well before bedtime. Children were being herded into bathtubs, and late arrivals were tossing hasty greetings to their neighbors as they dashed inside to join their kin. But here, in the thick of the residential area, they didn't have the rush of a passing breeze to keep them company while they waited for what would come next.

"Hey there, Sunny." A robust, dark haired gentleman came out of the stone-sided house with the enormous flowerbed next door. It was very hard to discern a Human's years. He was older than most the Micromales had seen; indelible lines were carved into the slacking skin of his face. He was still lean and muscular, and far too casually dressed in a long black robe over thin checkered house-pants, which threw their perception off that much further. He spoke a few more words in Pan Minor to accommodate the mixed company, but his accent was so thick that the visitors couldn't tell if he meant to greet them or warn them off.

"Uncle Barry, good afternoon." Sunduvall met him as he hopped the low hedge on the property line for a kiss on each cheek. The Micromales realized that they would have to excuse the lack of discretion that was the norm here.

"Don't you just keep getting prettier and prettier." He stroked her strawberry blonde bangs aside to see her full face, and they couldn't help but notice how overly tired his own face looked, as if he'd been fighting sleep to reach this moment. "Who're your friends?"

"These are my colleagues, Doctors Vladimir and Tendart of the Micromegt House of State's Left Hand." Sunduvall made the introductions, speaking much more calmly now that she was in familiar company.

"Barry Balmin, nice to meet you." He was versed enough in of Megt etiquette to know not to offer them his bare hand to shake. Instead, he placed his right open palm over his heart and lowered his eyes respectfully.

"Likewise, sir." Vladimir returned the same courtesy.

Barry caught Sunduvall's elbow and switched to a tongue that was every bit as indecipherable to the Micromales as the hieroglyphs on the clubhouse's sign. He obviously had something to say that was only for his niece's ears. The guttural purr of his deep voice hung like a threat in the air.

"I will rely on their opinion," she answered his question in Of Megt to keep her associates in the loop.

"Like we didn't see well, good, an' proof enough? C'mon, Sunny." Barry steered her back to the waiting men and swapped his secret language for the common tongue of Pan Minor with a great big smile and a much lighter tone. "Ha! Ha! Don't mind us none. Go on inside. I'll sit the first round out, but let me know how it goes."

"I will." She waved good-bye as they parted.

"One of your sire's others, I take it?" Vladimir asked just for his knowledge.

"A devil on his shoulder, to be sure." She led the men to the front door, which she opened without knocking.

"Daddy?"

"In the living room!" If they thought that the first accent they heard was strange, the loud tenor brogue that rang throughout the house didn't sound like real words at all. More like a song bent and forced into the structure of a language.

"*The speak*," Vladimir said in Tendart's mind, "*Methinks it is Chinese, though I have never heard it spoken in the living world*." He was something of a linguist in his own right, and had studied a few of the Earth's dead languages. Computerized voices hardly did justice to the natural tongue.

The group took the few steps from the front door around a short dividing wall into a wide-open space. It was adroitly portioned off to accommodate a cozy living room situated nicely before the expansive, casement bay window on the left and an unusually large, eight-piece, bar-stool seating arrangement at a long counter that segregated the kitchen. Everything was color-coordinated in cool, soothing shades of grey, blue and white. Natural wood added just enough of an eye-catching pop in accent pieces like the sofa table behind the couch where the only source of light in the room shone from a carved stone lamp, or the slab of aged timber that made for a very clever coffee table.

Although there was ample space for a dining set between the two areas, it was—oddly—left out of the thoughtful decor. In its place stood a large stainless steel block, a portable engine hoist, and an industrial tool chest that doubled as a sitting bench. The Micromales recognized the buzz of a sterile field. The configuration was slightly different, but they could tell that the rug under the predominant work area was an engineer's mat. They used such equipment in their own garage to absorb the chemical fuel from the cars they customized in their spare time.

The men paused in their tracks while Sunduvall cuddled the small figure that came out of a bedroom from the hallway beyond the common area. Another older man. Though he seemed slightly younger than the one they'd first met, his face was weighted with the same sort of leaden somnolence. He tied closed something that barely passed for a house robe over a bright white T-shirt and grey sweatpants. Bed clothes, but somehow he didn't strike them as the type to keep the hour.

"Hi, my Sunnyshine. Whose kids are these?" Steven grinned.

"Daddy." She dropped her tone as she stood in his arms. "This is the Left Hand. Remember that I told you I would bring them by?"

"I'm just pulling your leg, sweetie. Have a seat, everybody." He invited his guests to join them in the living room.

The Micromales sat in each one of the two white canvas club chairs, while Sunduvall joined her father on the microfiber slate grey sofa. With a stage so perfectly set, something extraordinary was bound to happen. A sense of the inevitable hung in the air, making it hard to break its spell with plain-spoken words.

"Good sire, I am Vladimir, and here is my other, Tendart. By your leave, may we know of your history?" He gathered that a rapid conduction of their business would be greatly appreciated.

"The whole ugly ball of wax, or just the sordid tale that led you boys to my door?" Steven teased.

"As much as you dare." Tendart readied his pad, and his nerves, to take notes.

"Firstly, are you a pure-blood Human?" Vladimir asked.

"Born and bred!" Steven laughed big then stopped short. "Well, I shouldn't say so like that considering how I'm a space orphan from birth. I dunno how many NAPS my dad, or his dad, took."

"Naps?"

"Nubile Alien Princesses."

"Daddy, anon!" Sunduvall was too late to block his words.

"To be sure." Vladimir swallowed. He intended to learn from his mistake of asking for clarification from this man. "So your full name is…?"

"Steven Rawley Sunduvall. Sunduvall's my real and honest surname. I gave it to my daughter so that, on record, she'd be called Sunduvall Sunduvall and it could become her legal house title carried by her line under of megt law. Poetic huh?"

"What of her gena?" Tendart could see where Sunduvall picked up her rambling way of speaking as he dared to venture into the midst of another loaded topic.

"I got Sunny out of a Maltrae demi-warrior back in the day before us dudes knew any better. Fools were lining up to take an alien bride after the Kazen Liberation. We used to think it was romantic—swooping down in a gleaming white Valefore to rescue the damsel—ball-swelling stuff like that…"

"Daddy!"

"…NEVER MIND that their own men didn't want 'em. That should've been the first hint right there; but what could you tell a sixteen-year-old, smart-ass, soldier boy that he didn't think he already knew?" Steven sighed whimsically, amused by his own past. "She used to beat on me. I found out quick how strong she was. We did battle off and on for fifteen years before I got to bury her. I didn't drop a tear at her funeral; and, I haven't called her name since the last time I was on top of her—"

"Daddy!" Sunduvall was going hoarse trying to chastise him.

"You're so touchy today, geez! It's not like I drew you a picture."

"Loose manners are what got you into this position, sir."

Steven mocked her openly.

Vladimir looked down at the floor, more certain than ever that there was no such thing as the Human's Hell, either out in the universe as a planet or as an incorporeal realm, since by now it hadn't opened up its maw to take back its escaped imp. "If I may…sire… you are sixty-five Human Years old?"

"Sorta for a few," Steven answered.

"Sort of?" Tendart wondered.

"Yeah." He gave no elaboration, just a carefree smile.

"W-while that is relatively advanced for a Human…" Vladimir found himself constantly needing to clear his throat just to get through the triage report. "…you appear as a rather much younger man, in sound condition. It is, however…*uncanny*…that a warrior would upon you unless she mistook your cloth. Were you thusly accosted?"

"By a woman? Hell no!" Steven drew back. "I've gone through a lot of things in my life, but I'll call it a day with a bullet if a woman ever put *that* on my resume. Warrior or not, she'd be meetin' her daddy drunk!"

Vladimir felt sorry for Sunduvall. She had a pathetic look on her face as if she, too, were wondering why the ground hadn't opened up to swallow her whole as an act of mercy. Her father was vivacious and alive in a way that men could ill afford to be in this day, yet still he wore his years. Hard living had kept his body slim, but the weight of it showed in everything from scars to crow's feet. His more-salt-than-pepper hair was modernly styled—possibly too much so—in a messy rat-tail of curls and straight bits wound up at the back of his head. Some manner of drawn art ran up both of his arms from the fingertips and under the ragged ends of the threadbare terry cloth bathrobe that he was lightly wrapped in. He was an endless source of pause, just like everything else in this strange village.

"Anon, kind sire." Vladimir meant that. Steven may have been wild with the heat of ribaldry but it was clear that he loved his daughter above all else. Throughout their cringe-worthy confab he periodically held her hand to comfort her as if it were the most natural thing to do. Fathers who raised their daughters in the conventions of the of megt understood that it wasn't the will of the code to keep open lines of affection, or pass so many unnecessary overly-familiar words.

They'd known Sunduvall for many Human Years, and had assumed things that were now proven untrue. They could never have imagined that such a staunch traditionalist had deep, eclectic roots that weren't at all of megt. It made her kind and understanding—and most obviously patient.

"If it is not just so then what else could it be?" Vladimir asked, conversant with the need of some men to be eased along. Somehow the day was never late enough, and facts were never clear enough to belay the surprise of an unanticipated parturiency.

"C'mon, guys. You're kids but you're not babies." Steven rolled his eyes. "In your line of work I'm sure you've seen enough of it to know better."

"We have doctored all make and manner, but we have never attended the likes of you." Tendart tried to get back on the clinical straight and narrow. "We must completely understand, most especially now that stranger things have happened."

"You mean those abductions in the Valley?" Steven caught on. "Well, don't worry. This was an old-fashioned fuckup. Me and the boys were out spending a bit o' the bank."

"Oh my Elders, the things you say. Must you?" Sunduvall lamented.

"I'm sorry, Sunny, but I get a bit lonely sometimes. I didn't mean for it to be anything more than a harmless round of fun. Other guys do it. Jake's a regular in the Cat House…"

"Uncle Jake is not of your cloth, Daddy!" She blew up. "What care have you whatever he does? Where is he now, as you sit here *alone* in your hour?"

"I can call 'im over if you wanna yell at us both."

"Daddy!"

"Okay! Jokes aside. I've been sick for a while. Just sick. I'm not as young as I used to be!" For the first time in their conversation Steven looked nervous. "Look…I didn't tell my girl, but the doctors here said that I had come down with HTB. I was treated, and I thought that I was shored up or else I wouldn't have gone out that night."

"Habitare Tuberculosis, another serious bout of acclimation sickness so soon, *again*? And you kept that from me?"

"Because I know how you worry. Please. It's apt that all this is just a residual side effect of the treatment. You dragged these boys out here for nothing."

"How I would fervently pray that it is so, yea, I cannot. I have seen your symptoms and I recognize them. Please submit yourself to be examined."

"I can see my own doctor."

"But you won't. You slink and hide away in here pretending not to be at home when the attendants come by."

"How would you know?"

"Uncle Barry told me so. He is equally as concerned and, quite frankly, equally as culpable."

"Why? He didn't knock me up."

"DAD-DY."

"All right, then!" He was tired of arguing. "Far be it from me to waste these boys' time anymore than it's already been. Let's get to it."

"What symptoms have you noted?" Tendart asked.

"I saw his *rude awakening* for myself. You could imagine how surprised I was." She used the vernacular to keep her father in the loop of what was going to be an increasingly more clinical conversation from here on out. "It drove him frail to where he was unconscious for the better part of the day. I performed as much of the standard examination as I dared. Upon palpitation of the lower abdominal vault, I detected the first stage formation of the utheria—"

"Or a tumor," Steven injected.

Sunduvall ignored him. "I took a blood sample into the lab and it tested positive for the presence of the X-Minus Chromosome. That was two days ago. I would have called upon you sooner, but this sir for me left world."

"I was on duty."

"You found a way to hide from me! If it were not for Uncle Fran grounding you until you are medically cleared you would not be here right now!" She swung away from him, determined not to be sucked into another pointless back and forth. "I am desperate for a second opinion."

"'Tis to you, sire. May we examine you?" Vladimir needed Steven's final word. Even though they had made his acquaintanceship at his daughter's behest, this was the one area in life where warriors had no true say or sway.

"Does Sunny have to watch? I'm a bit embarrassed." Steven blushed.

"Now? Really?" she jibed. "*Suddenly*?"

"Since she is your warrior, we will treat her as such and bade her patience while we go into privacy."

"Good!" Steven hopped right up. "Well then, my warrior, I shall return," he teased Sunduvall in an Of Megt cant as he led his new doctors to his bedroom.

"The better for it, I hope." She shot back.

Night.
Centaurus Wall.
The *Southerland*.

There should have been an alarm to go along with the gasp that was heard all throughout the UEDF. Jackson Hill waited for any bit of news, but nothing beyond the standard mission reports came in. It was as if it were an ordinary deployment on another unspectacular day, just business as usual. His flight of Valefore Fighters that were attached to the No Quarter retrieval mission had been repurposed to escort the Medical Corps emergency response team back to One. That seemed to be the extent of the hitches and glitches. There was no reply to his request for a site forensics report. A bare-bones investigation was possibly underway—or already hastily concluded—and most disquieting, there was no word of Captain Hjorth's condition. He'd written an action plan for the investigation into the disappearance of the Crazy Eights that lingered unacknowledged—even unwanted. Dr. Parvati Galleon was put in charge of the entire mission with a full discretion order from higher up to make her authority absolute. He had tried to contact her several times, but all of his update inquiries were met with two small words: *stand by*. It made his heart sick to be on the outside staring in at an unapologetic cover-up.

He raked his hands through his dirty-blond hair for the umpteenth time trying to recall if he'd ever seen a bald Yomin. He was sure he was going to pull every single strand out of his own head before this ordeal was over and he would have liked some assurance that it would grow back. He checked his inbox and then his watch as he stood away from his desk. By now, he was well aware of the fact that he had been left out of the loop on purpose. If hope was his only sustenance he would have starved to death. There was no point delaying any further.

Jackson crept quietly down the short hallway to look in on his sleeping daughter. The spindly tweenie was sprawled out as if she'd been struck down by sleep, which was usually the case. Lee Hill was a girl too eager for leisure. Everything she did was full force and without circumspection. Even a little thing like getting ready for bed became a dramatic stage performance of his drudgingly reiterated commands and her pleading for five more minutes right up until the moment that sleep snuck up on her. He smiled victoriously as he positioned her comfortably so that all of her limbs were on the bed, and tucked the covers in around her. She'd sleep through the night without ever realizing that he had left.

Evening.
Earth.
Solito Lake Retirement Village.

This really was quite a case. Tendart completed the physical examination for the forth time while Vladimir put the blood work in for a third run. Their findings were disturbingly conclusive. This old man was gravid.

"Okay. I'm going to read that look on your face as bad news." Steven broke the silence that had held the room for nearly the entire examination. "I'm dying."

Tendart's eyes sprung to Steven's face, wide with shock, wondering if he was joking again or was just that mired in denial.

"I knew it." Steven sighed. "A man can't piss a cup of blood a day for weeks and think anything else. I didn't tell Sunny about that. This is going to kill her."

Vladimir floated over with the test results in hand to quickly throw some much-needed clarity over the situation. "Sire, you are breeding. And while that is a stressful state for your aged body, it is not inherently fatal."

"You're kidding."

"See for yourself." Vladimir handed him the medi-pad. The positive finding was clear enough for a layman to read. "The symptoms of this, your first conception, are typical. Within twenty hours of successful implantation you had a bloody show; and, the subsequent lettings over the course of the past three weeks was your body repurposing your organs and developing what was merely rudimentary material in Human males into a nutrient rich environment around the embryo…"

"Wait, wait, this is… *what*?" Steven couldn't let the Micromegt doctor go on spouting information, as if he were reading passages out of a textbook, in the face of his life-changing shock. Up until now he'd been endulging his dramatic daughter, only half-listening to her for days, all the while believing in a deeper sort of worst than the writ-large fact of the matter he held in his hands.

He scanned the room, feeling surrounded by panes of glass. They just slipped out of the ether in dramatic slow motion, crashing with a deafening shriek one after another. He stared at the doctors, utterly amazed by how they could mill about so calmly on top of all that broken glass. He was standing perfectly still, yet the shards had cut him wide open. Sheet after sheet, each stained with a pivotal instance of his long colorful life, ignominiously destroyed until there was nothing left but a visceral horror and fading disbelief. How could he feign ignorance with his entire existence lying smashed at his feet and the proof positive in his clutches? Everything was revealed, and he could no longer deny how he had ruined himself beyond retrieve.

Chapter 3 ————————————————

Night.
Sculptor Void.
The *Thresher*.

Jackson Hill paced the length of his Valfore star jet as he waited in the private bay that he pulled many favors to gain access to. Aside from *Venomous'* landing lights, the tiny hangar was pitch black–which was hardly a factor for his acute Yomin senses. His arrival on the *Thresher* had to stay a secret for as long as possible. There were forces already hard at work trying to turn one of the most shocking acts of violence against a UEDF officer into a bit of misinterpreted COM chatter.

Bad news traveled fast in the small arena of high command. Even before he left the Southerland the quandary of Captain Hjorth had a clearance level and a hush code, per Dr. Galleon's orders. The Medical Corps was on high alert at the Main hospital in One City; the TAU unit that handled the No Quarter recovery was called home to One. After all of his requests for a mission status update were blatantly ignored, Jackson knew that the captain's wife was going to be left with nothing except questions and no husband for days, weeks, months, or even years if he didn't act fast.

The plight of one soldier could never be allowed to affect the well-being of the UEDF. The most powerful standing army in the galaxy had to be properly feared—at least that was the popular consensus. If word spread that a brazen, unknown enemy predated on a Norid squadron while they were out on maneuvers without consequence, morale would decline; and certainly rival forces would move against them.

The Nation Fleet had only one true leader, the supreme command general, and he was already working his magic. The cover-up began the instant he sicced Dr. Galleon on Captain Hjorth. He would have ordered the Muu transport to be destroyed, if so many escape pods hadn't gotten away. The general always said that a certain level of atrocity had to be endured. He wasn't an evil man, just a soul hardened by the cruelty that had scarred him. He'd shed his blood to make the UEDF strong enough to keep the Nation Fleet safe, and he meant for that supremacy to continue after he was gone. Yet how could it when the same cruelty that had forged him was still out there just as thirsty as ever? It hadn't been at all subdued. It had grown more greedy and devious in the century since a lasting peace was forged between most of the civilized worlds. The general had a unique understanding of this truth and he alone stood willing to do battle with all of his vigor, assets, flaws, and limitations on display. Self-actuated transparency—though the view was bleak, and ugly at times—was his best quality.

Jackson didn't often agree with him, but he respected him. He knew for certain that the general only ever had their collective best interest in mind. It was just that sometimes following along blindly wasn't the right thing to do. Sometimes the greater good could only be served by a dose of bitter reality. They all would have to fight, not just accept the sacrifice of one man. Leaving the Southerland when he did was every bit as orchestrated as the information blackout was against him. Jackson didn't want to be available to receive the general's orders. As a point admiral, he had the autonomy to act. Only a direct command from the seat of the UEDF's supreme command general could quell him. He wouldn't let that happen until he had delivered his message and set in motion a chain of events that even the general's omnipotent power couldn't whitewash.

Jackson turned toward the source of a light noise—the barest rustling of fabric and padded knees dragging through the maintenance ducts hidden behind the smooth plated panels of the bulkhead. The small, lithe figure of a man slipped out of a three-foot-square sliding door trying to control the precarious bundle in his arms. His fallow brown skin blended in with the shadows, but the overabundance of metal in his large crystal-blue eyes made them glow like hot coals long after he'd stepped away from the lit access duct.

"Elders, Beau! You sure took your time," he snapped at the elfin demi-male.

"Sorry, Pia kept wantin' to know why I needed a set of full robing when I was on duty." Beau trained his flashlight on Jackson before tossing over the ball of clothes.

"Whatja tell her?" He wasn't keen on of megt clothing. On the other hand, nothing else could serve as a more perfect disguise. A properly sheathed man in public was beyond reproach. No one would dare to stop or question him. Even other men would be remiss to address him without being able to tell who he was underneath all of the cloth."

"Not a damn thing, dude, don't worry." He dismissed Jackson's nosiness. "You sure Navaho didn't pick you up on radar when you snuck up on us?"

"I'm sure."

"You've got the better part of ten minutes before Chief Reed figures out that this bay is active. This whole part of the ship's supposed to be dark. Why all the slippin' an' slidin'? Just an admiral's pleasure?"

"I wish I could tell you, but I don't want you mixed up in the wreckage."

"That ol' bastard's makin' his last days in office real memorable, huh? I heard how Lord Vahe got called in. I guess we're gonna get the news soon that he's out of the race for the seat. Not that I wanna serve under another scary bastard, but all the same."

"How, for the love of it, is everybody hearin' all of everythin' except for me?" Jackson grunted angrily as he bullied his way through the task of wrapping himself up in the many layers of robing as quickly as he could. Apparently the UEDF was running quite tidily without him. He decided to leave what he knew was the long reach of the general alone. "Never mind. Things might get hot, you've gotta hang back with nothin' to say no matter what happens."

"Uh oh, sounds like the General's gunnin' for me, too."

"Yeah, well, he hates the Horde like Humans hate the Devil. Anything's everything in times like these."

"Wow, that made my head hurt."

"I'll let myself out." He set his watch's timer.

"Glao, I'll keep everybody distracted on the bridge. I've got a deck full of hotshot young ensigns just lookin' for any way to shine their brass. Catchin' an admiral by the toe would be pure fun for 'em. Safe go."

"Thanks, Captain. Here's hopin'."

Ella peered at the door's monitor. She wasn't expecting anyone, let alone the fully-sheathed male who stood waiting for her to answer. Anyone could have been under that length of cloth. She wondered if she had forgotten something out of the lab's daily report that made Lieutenant Yeji have to send one of her husbands over to collect the paperwork. She opened the door and the male rushed right in. She nearly screamed before she realized that it would be a futile act—the walls were soundproof.

"What do you want?!" She groped for an impromptu weapon, another exercise in futility considering that any of megt male worth his water wouldn't be felled by anything short of lethal force.

"Ella, it's me." Jackson uncovered his face.

"Jackie?" She was more alarmed after she recognized him. "What's going on?"

"You didn't hear this from me, understand? You need to contact Dr. Galleon and ask about Aaron."

"Wh-what? I don't—"

"There's been a raid or somethin'. The Crazy Eights are MIA, all save for Aaron. He was found on a Muu transport steamin' for Godgin II, tampered with an' disabled. No matter what else you hear, that's all the truth of it we know until Aaron can tell us any different."

"Disabled…how?…Jackson." She choked on her words as the shock began to weaken her composure.

"Now's not the time for tears. He's alive an' you need to be on Galleon's doorstep makin' some noise. Don't take no for an answer. Get Virginia Bay involved if you have to." He comforted her in the little time he had left. "I gotta go. Don't waste a minute after I walk out this door. Call Galleon an' hop on the next thing flyin' her way."

"This has the Generals' stink all over it."

"He didn't strike the match, but he'll do what he thinks is best to put it out."

"I understand…thank you."

Evening.
Earth.
Solito Lake Retirement Village.

Steven spoke Of Megt fluently, but for the life of him he couldn't follow the conversation that his daughter was having with his brand new doctors. Something was happening apart from what was already going on inside of him.

He didn't know much about the Earth's culture, though he knew better than to judge it by the weirdness he'd seen on TV. In the handful of years since he moved into the village, he hadn't spent more than three days consecutively on-world. Every time he came home there seemed to be something going on in the community at large beyond the peace and safety of his gated haven. Civil demonstrations were an everyday affair, while public-service announcements—that had the distinct ring of anti-alien propaganda—ran like commercials between shows broadcasting day and night. Still, none of it was of any concern to him at the time. Steven wished that he had paid more attention, especially now that he was hearing funny English words like *Recidivist* and *Law Malfeasant*. He really didn't know what *expansion* was, but his daughter intended to schedule him for it the very day he was *scrambled*. He'd only ever heard of scrambling through crude jokes. Exactly what that did that involve? It didn't sound any more pleasant than *expansion*. Both seemed like something that should be done to morning eggs, not to a living person. Why was the entire prognosis coated with a thick skin of disaster?

Then it came to him. Maybe this was the end. He could really be dying. All that perplexing doctor-speak could be his daughter desperately reaching for some extraordinary measure that would save his life. She loved him too much to let him go without a fight. He'd lived in the shadow of death for so long that the only thing that could surprise him at this point was the form it took. He accepted the risk of being a fighter pilot and knew the end would come sans forewarning. Space was dangerous. The UEDF's enemies were merciless. Even without the threat of war, there was the violence of an active universe and the deep still of the void that was always calling to him. Nothing else seemed as real as that. Only the love of his daughter had ever been able to pull him away from what he'd both loved and struggled with his whole life long until this very moment. Steven sat at his counter in his little white house on a strange planet, possibly terminally ill, imagining that he could hear the soprano trill of his dead wife's voice calling his name, while a funny churning in his gut made him feel like throwing up.

"Please understand. My father is not as Human as the Humans who are native to this world," Sunduvall expounded on a scribble she'd written in the margin of her notes, just in case it made a difference in how the Hand approached her father's care. "His lab work will say so, yea having been born in deep space hath altered his physiology. Greater lung volume, uneven strength-to-weight ratio, colder blood, and a high threshold for pain. Even his age is merely an estimation, though he is past his middle years. He is hale and hardy in ways that are unusual, but that is not always a credit in his favor. Aside from the short while he spent on Mars, this last six months have been the longest he has ever been downed. E'en so, his occupation requires a great deal of off-world travel. I suspect that is why he had fallen to another bout of HTB recently."

"Indeed. The constant readjustment to the planet's environment is a perennial burden," Vladimir agreed. "Can he not take time away from such labors? This quick will be ordeal enough without the danger of avoidable illnesses."

"What must happen now?" Sunduvall chose not to comment on her colleague's suggestion while her father was within earshot. He'd been polite—for the most part—and surprisingly quiet since the examination, but that would change in a shocking instance if he realized that they were discussing the one thing he had done without fail, aside from loving her, as if it were a frivolous hobby.

"'Tis to you, warrior. In a way it is fortuitous that your sire resides in this refuge apart from society. Perchance a *silence* can be maintained that would spare him the wonted dramatic alterations."

"He will rail against any attempt to corral him. As a doctor I have treated the product of human cruelty. A man such as my own could not survive the bitter review of this hateful earth. He must be scrambled."

"Then I will consult with my others as to how to proceed."

Chapter 4————————————————————

Night.
Maduro Grand.
The *Solace*, Isolation Pod.

"Remarkable." Dr. Galleon stood in awe of the scientific mystery that had fallen into her lap.

Captain Aaron Hjorth lay deep in the sleep of stasis, packaged for the trip to One City. The youthful sheen on his face paled against the data she'd already gleaned from his blood work. There was an interesting tale to be told, if the general let her tell it. Someone had gone to great lengths with much more of a reason beyond enthusiastic sadism against a hated foe. The clothes she cut off of him were hand sewn for a physical build of his general size, though no married man would have chosen an all-white kuffiya; that was a garment for virgins. If he had scuttled his squad mates and plotted his defection there certainly were easier ways to go about it; however, that was an unwarranted stretch. Some other party was most definitely involved and the captain, unfortunately, fell victim to a crime that didn't necessarily have his name on it.

"Would you say that he's been scrambled?" She turned to Dr. Ricki with a knowing smile.

"I wouldn't take that kind of a guess." Ricki answered sparingly.

"I thought you Yomin knew your own." Galleon didn't blame her collegue for her guarded posture. She had always been short with her. There was something in Ricki's faining untra-femininity that rubbed her the wrong way.

"We Yomin are more skeptical than most."

"You are familiar with the process of veddification, though."

"In theory."

"It's the most stable form of DNA replacement, but it's a long process. Captain Hjorth was only unaccounted for for a few hours. That's not time enough to complete the Vedda Protocol, which was clearly the aim."

"Do you have the results?"

"I'm posting the initial findings as we speak." Galleon hit send on a very abbreviated report. "The series began with a crude scrambler that contained the key components of the old Yomin POW Veddification series. From there it turns to a hodgepodge of narcotics and guesswork. It's really quite fascinating. I'm going to be studying him for—"

"Doctor, you don't mean what you're about to say." A bit of alarm spiked Ricki's tone.

"I'll study him only as a patient. Of course he'll be awake and aware and everything else, but don't expect too much from him. It's likely that he's completely mad. I don't know how I'm going to break that news to his wife, let alone the General."

"It's too soon to say so."

Galleon chuckled as if she were speaking to an amusing house pet. "Oh, Ricki, were you anything more than a pretty face, I would elaborate; but your masters didn't program you for critical thinking. Just as his would-be masters wanted to create an obedient, docile puppet. At least that much is obvious. What would be the point of going to all this trouble otherwise? Your masters came up with a process to be able to safely contain and interrogate their enemies. What better way to accomplish that than by turning a prisoner of war into one of you very basic, agreeable creatures? Don't you see?"

Ricki bit her tongue. It took every ounce of her acumen, and a reserve of common sense she didn't know she had, to retreat to her calm place. She reminded herself that Meruvians were notoriously — and often unintentionally — hard to work with. It wasn't Dr. Galleon's fault that she was born with a primitive brain, any more than it was her own for being a Yomin clone. Ricki loved her job; more so, she loved having the freedom to choose to do a job that she wanted and trained for. Her caste classification as an Aoede Muse naturally led to her joining the Medical Corps. But people like Dr. Galleon, who didn't understand the Yomin condition, often mistook a common evolution of an already-practiced skill for biological programming. She really wondered how someone so biased would be able to help Captain Hjorth with his recovery, or if she intended to see him recovered at all.

"Aren't you due back on the *Southerland*?" Dr. Galleon asked out of nowhere.

"I'm meeting Nan in One. We're going to take the ride together. Why?"

"With Captain Whip?"

"No. The debriefing is going to take more hours than we can spare."

"You're mistaken. The exit reports have already been sent to the General. The Last Rites are probably only going to spend ten on the ground before they turn back."

"B…but…We haven't completed Captain Hjorth's examination. You just said it yourself that only the initial findings are in."

"The General gave me full discretion."

"Discretion? What does that mean?"

"What it means, my dear, is that I will act as I see fit to preserve our interests and report only to the General, as per his request. Why must every little thing be spelled out for you people?"

"I'm concerned for the Captain."

"Well, then it's a lucky thing for both of us that you'll soon be an outside consultant. You can happily go back to your warm cocoon on the Southerland without a care to furrow that pretty brow. Do I have to give you written orders, or can I count on your professionalism?"

Ricki stared at the pathetic shadow of a man whose lively laugh used to brighten the darkest mood. He needed a champion, but her hands were already tied. He deserved better than he was about to receive, but the general's word was absolute law. Tears came too easily to the eyes of muses, her heart bled too readily. She could imagine the satisfaction that swelled Dr. Galleon's ego as she took her uncontrollable biological response to the suffering of another as a sign of weakness. She braced for the predictable dig that she could already see forming on Galleon's thin chapped lips.

"Maybe you should rest. We won't reach One until morning. I've scheduled an early staff meeting to put together a team to handle Captain Hjorth's case around the clock. You see? I haven't forgotten my oath. So rest easy, okay?"

"All right," Ricki took the out knowing that it was the better part of valor, and that using her muse skill to destroy her superior's mind was the only thing that could make her feel better right now.

"Good. I'll see you at first light, then," Galleon said, though it wasn't necessary; she'd already won. The last word always had to go to her.

Night.
Earth.
Base 7, Allied Defense Force (ADF) Housing.

"A unique case has fallen to us." Vladimir saved their most controversial patient for the end of the day's case review. The rest of the Left Hand fell quiet at the table waiting on his words as he pulled up the file. "An aged Human in a retirement village stands three weeks in and driven."

Nothing.

Not a single sound. Not out of Tendart's younger brother, Tyran, who was lively enough for any sort of outburst; or from Jaylen, who hardly ever held his tongue. Etitus just sat there as if he hadn't heard a thing; along with Tendart—who seemed to be pretending that he had nothing to do with the case at all.

Etitus' son, Gier, had a sort of unbelieving expression on his face that mirrored Mect's and Yemeer's, but none of them put a voice to it. Min pulled a tight frown and hid it under the privacy of his kuffiya. Sage looked at his brother, Span, and smiled—only the Elders on high knew what was behind that picture-perfect smile. Knowing him, it was something off-color and a bit too Yomin for polite company.

Finally—after carefully turning Vladimir's statement over in his mind—their leader, Span, managed two words: "You say?"

And with that the floodgates opened.

"How now?" Tyran fished for reiteration.

"But how is that so?" Yemeer wanted details.

"What manner of *she-beast* could have committed such a crime?" Min wanted to know a few things as well.

"'Tis by his own purchase, literally," Tendart finally spoke up.

"The knavery," Jaylen spat. "Wretched brute. Glao and for shame."

"Good Elders, how rotten is his cloth?" Sage asked a pertinent question, free of shock, but not of his wicked smile.

"Sixty-five Human Years by the count of the Earth, but less by the stroke of his origins in deep space." Vladimir didn't quite know how to answer.

"May his Devil take him. How will he survive the quick?" Jaylen was already leery of the patient's chances.

"He is healthy and cut of sterner stuff than the Humans born here. Though he is set to break in. That alone may kill him."

"We think to arrange an expansion posthaste, but the law requires that all Human males who have transgressed thusly be reported and scrambled. It must be considered that his extraterrestrial physiology may not be compatible with the standard panacea." Tendart flashed a frown at his brother. He already had to smack Tyran's hand away from his neat files that he'd been steadily picking to pieces since the revelation of the day sank in.

"Did his blood test Human?" Tyran asked what he'd already gleaned from his rummaging, which he continued in spite of Tendart's protestation.

"In a manner of speaking, for all intents and purposes." Vladimir waved an uncertain gesture. "We know that scramblers only work on Humans. If he is not enough of one, or some sort of subspecies, then who knows what it could do to him."

"His daughter, Dr. Sunduvall, is prepared to take the risk," Tendart added.

"The genetic resequencing alone may cause him to slip the quick," Sage spoke. "Scrambling is far too invasive by design. It is something of a punishment above all. Whate'er benefits it has are far outweighed by the risks."

"Then once again we will aside the law," Jaylen agreed with a satisfied nod. He didn't like being forced to do the Human League's dirty work.

"He must be expanded. If we attend him without disclosure, we would be putting him at risk. If for any reason throughout his care we must utilize an outside resource, it would be impossible to explain such a blatant flouting of the law. Not all agencies are as willing to defy the Human League." Vladimir would have loved nothing more than to be able to thumb his nose at the ignorance that had pried its way into their profession; but he had to put the welfare of their patient first.

"You could gradually administer the scrambler." An idea suddenly dawned on Mect. "Stagger its effects to allow him to develop a tolerance. We have tailored such medicines before, I do not see why we could not design a scrambler that would work on his unique biology."

"Would you like to make it?" Tendart asked only as a formality. Mect was already busily writing down the formulas that were racing through his mind nearly faster than he could catch them.

"Gladly," he answered with pep in his voice. "For the novelty of it alone."

Chapter 5 —————————————————

Evening.
Earth.
Base 7, Allied Defense Force (ADF) Housing.

Sunduvall's life changed the morning that her father passed out in his front yard. He collapsed to the ground, and she felt the world shift beneath her feet. She sat in her study replaying the moment over and over again trying to find an answer for that one haunting question: What could she have done differently?

If she had come over the day before when he asked her to drive him to the supermarket outside of the village, perhaps he wouldn't have been up to venturing into the valley that night.

She spent as much time with him as his lifestyle would allow. After her stepmother died Sunduvall had hoped that he would come to live with her, but that was too hard to even suggest with her beloved uncles surrounding him. His running buddies, her caregivers when she was a child, her family, the Horde. They were notorious throughout the UEDF and becoming increasingly so every day that they lived on Earth. She was well aware of this, yet she did nothing but dare to hope.

That fateful morning her father caught her just as she was coming home from work. He woke up at 5:00 a.m. Universal Time on the dot every able day of his life. So it didn't surprise her to receive a call from him at 1:35 a.m. Earth Time. She could hear tiredness, and possibly the remains of a hangover, in his voice. She asked about his health in spite of what she suspected. He offered her a sugar-coated response—just as sweet as the lollipops he brought for her children—that she knew better than to accept; but she was too tired to bicker after her long shift.

With the knowledge that she would soon see the truth of his well-being for herself, Sunduvall told him she'd come over to take him shopping at eight in the morning and let that be the end of it.

Her second mistake was giving him time to organize a plan. He didn't like doctors to the point of his own detriment. She already knew, as she looked in on her children and climbed into bed beside her husband, that her father would have his game face on when she got to his house.

He had hours to shore himself up, and he appeared to be in fine fettle by the time she arrived. His blood pressure, temperature, and lung volume were all normal across the board, though he did seem a little slow. She checked his vitals twice before they left, and by the time they returned she had convinced herself that he was merely suffering from aftereffects of some cringe-worthy, epic celebration complete with vice and booze far beyond the propriety of a man of his station. She intended to have a talk with him about that after the day's errands were run. No doubt it would be a jolly back and forth, full of comedy and thin denials closed out with a vague promise to try to be good—or at least less obvious—in the future.

She was ready to be pacified when she parked her car in his driveway again. He took the bag he'd been holding on his lap and fished his keys out of his pocket as he shuffled toward the front door. Sunduvall went around to open the trunk of her grey sedan where the bulk of the shopping lay. It did pause her a bit that her father wasn't instantly at her side trying to snatch up all of the bags. In spite of the ten-times-over-his strength in her body, he was still too much of an old fashioned gentleman to let any lady fill her arms with things to carry, let alone his own and only daughter. She glanced his way. He was still—oddly—leafing through the ring of keys weighing out which one of the three was the one he needed. That struck her as unusual, but a greeting from her Uncle Barry had drawn her attention away just long enough for her to miss her father's initial swoon.

A soundless, perpetual, hanging instance. The only movement in the entire world was her father's limp body slumping into the bushes at the foot of his front porch. She hadn't drawn enough of a breath to sustain the primal scream that tore out of her throat. Her uncle had already jumped over the low hedge between their houses and was turning Steven over before she managed to make her rubbery legs work. How she admonished herself for her hysterical panic! She was a damned doctor, after all. She was trained to react on a dime to a crisis. Here she was faced with the biggest emergency of her life, and all she could show for her years of faithful practice was a layman's paralyzed state of shock.

She'd skinned both of her knees on the cool concrete as she flew to his side to examine him. He wasn't dead, not even unconscious; in fact he was fighting to turn over back toward the bushes. His pulse was so strong that she could see it pounding through the thin skin of his neck. If he wasn't having a heart attack, then what was he doing?

Her very last—and possibly the most embarrassing— moment of denial came as she recoiled thinking that he was only being sick just before he heaved at least two pints of bright red blood out in one go. A few drops escaped the dirt beneath the bushes dotting the walkway as her father wilted to his side. It was as tidy as it could possibly be, much more so than she had ever seen it before. In her line of work this was an everyday occurrence that didn't merit a doctor's visit. It was a natural thing meant to herald a change in the body; and, though she was stunned, she wasn't as completely caught off guard as she wished she'd been once the many clues came rushing back to taunt her.

Uncle Barry muttered something in Polish. He wasn't surprised in the least, which nearly led her to question him right there and then, but she was the first responder on the scene with a priority to tend to her patient.

Her father had fully drifted out of consciousness before they could get him into his bedroom. Sunduvall didn't approve of his modern human wardrobe. Jeans were cumbersome devices, nearly impossible to remove from a prone position. She would have cut them off him but she didn't dare, considering that he never wore any undergarments.

She pulled his blood-spotted T-shirt up just far enough to palpate the abdominal vault. At this point, there was no use pretending that she didn't know exactly what was going on. Uncle Barry was slowly unlacing her father's combat boots as she completed the initial exam. Her father never had much meal or weight. He was small, barely five foot seven, with not an ounce of fat. His good condition couldn't account for the hard-packed, bright pink lump that sat just under his navel. It was as tough and unyielding as the round top of a baseball. Her uncle stood concerned; they were in complete concert.

He asked why Steven was unconscious.

She offered that it was because of the shock to his system.

She asked if her father had been drinking.

Barry answered, not so much in the past few days.

She wanted to ask about their activities. Just before she could, her uncle freely admitted that they'd been in the valley all last night. There were thirty-six hours in a universal day, a full thirty-six and a half hours ahead of Earth's time. She did the math in her head to home in on a time of insemination. Twenty hours had to have passed between then and now. But, when her uncle gave up that Steven had only the one partner—a slight Yomin with a moon face and dull eyes, in the middle of her cusp turnaround—Sunduvall completely lost the clinical detachment that she had so desperately tried to cling to and demanded to know why any man would pay for sex with a demi-female who was at her most potent.

She stopped him from answering. She didn't want to learn the truth as gently and as reasonably as he'd put it, fearing that it would make sense to even her, the daughter of the suddenly fragile old man stretched out unconscious.

The Nation Fleet had quickly accepted the reality of the of megt races and what co-mingling with them could bring. Almost from the moment of first contact there'd been sires no matter how many guidelines the UEDF created. The blending of their species enriched their lives. She would have never been born if not for the open, progressive arms of Humans who understood that real strength came from unity—but things were not so cohesive here on Earth.

These Humans had only met the of megt and demi races thirty-odd years ago. They recoiled with all the fear, confusion, and irrational loathing of a long-isolated society that had never imagined such differences were possible. The Human men of Earth were the self-proclaimed masters of the universe who didn't like being challenged in any way. Warriors, and all of their demi derivatives, were a direct affront to their masculinity. They were far too seductive to ignore, being beautiful on the whole and amiable even under the worst circumstances.

It was often said that there was a warrior to suit every man's fantasy: whether he preferred tall blondes or tiny brunettes; gently blushing blossoms with voices as sweet as honey; or riotous quick-tempered vixens who could party with the best, he could find the embodiment of his ideal woman in both looks and temperament. It was only the race that offered something of an obstacle.

Of megt races, like the Akkut and the Micromegts, tended to be very conservative and code minded. That was often enough to keep the vast majority of them out of frivolous liaisons. True demis were very mindful about whom they mated with. They were wrapped tightly in rigid codes of conduct and a general distaste for Humans. In spite of all their extraordinary differences, none of the of megt could hold a candle to the genetic diversity of the Yomin. Nature was deliberate; codes were restrictive; but the Yomin were all-inclusive in both their own genome, and with their advanced DNA replacement technology.

Long before any of the races currently populating the Earth ever heard of them, the Yomin set out to engineer a caste of demi-warriors in the hopes that injecting of megt blood into their species would turn the tide of war back in their favor. There were many distinct advantages that they'd hoped to gain, but their plans were too little too late to bear fruit. The Yomin fell, leaving behind entire castes of new, half-warrior creations that quickly became the bane of entire worlds.

They could hide what they were better than most. They didn't have the tell-tale of megt markers—pointed ears, noticeable height, or great strength. To Human men, they seemed as normal as their own women, both outside and inside. The Yomin were at the pitch of their guile when they designed a woman who could carry her own child, and then at times pass along the egg. They had assured the perpetuation of their manufactured race with that little gem. Such women were not only easy on any eye, they were uninhibited with a nearly predatory urge to mate when they were at their most potent. Men who didn't know any better could mistake their drive for a healthy appetite. That's why they made such good prostitutes. Brothels hired them by the score generation after generation—sisters, mothers, daughters. Since the average Yomin on Earth only lived around ten years, the market never became flooded with worn-out products. It was the harsh, unforgiving, reality of life on a planet that had the luxury to turn flesh into a commodity.

It hurt Sunduvall to her soul when she thought about how her own father had waded into the mire to return as a victim of his own deviation. He should have never come here. There were no such temptations in the Nation Fleet. He would have been better off serving in the UEDF all his life and taking his last breath in the cockpit of his Valefore. Anything less was pure avoidable folly. Everything else was a waste.

At the end of that portentous day she looked at her uncle then down at her father and saw how human they really were in their ignorance, their arrogance, and their mistakes. They were both long-time horn donners, well practiced in the art of conquest. Paying for sex was just another thing to try. She knew they had been doing it almost from the minute that they'd stepped foot on Earth. Just as well as she knew that her gentle, loving, flawed father was lying in the darkest hour of his life with his ability to survive in serious question because she failed him as his warrior-daughter.

That was the missed link in the chain of events that had forever changed their small world. Her father's indescretion would be a moment's gossip in their progressive Nation Fleet. Embarrassing, pitiful, possibly disruptive on a small ship, and likely cause enough for a temporary rotation out of theater; but ultimately their private cross to bear—a point her father could argue alone and win any day of the week. But here on the Earth, it was a crime to the Humans, and a dereliction of her duty as a warrior to have a male of her house be found scandalous. She was obligated by the Micromegt code she had adopted to see to his wellness. Instead she indulged him, allowed him to burn up his own life. By of megt law, the men of warriors could not be held in account. Whatever he did or suffered was caused by her lack of control over her house. This was her shame to bear, not his, and it was killing her slowly.

She had sat with him until he woke up. He was feeling much better and ready to dismiss every single word of the ordeal that was described to him with all of its gory details intact. Her uncle shrugged and went home to eat dinner. He knew better than to try to convince Steven of anything when he was in full-on stubborn mode. She'd hardly gotten out half of what she'd meant to say above her father's fierce insistence that everything was fine. He talked her right out the door. She had to go to work, but she returned just as soon as she could catch him on world with the Hand in tow.

That was the sum of her past week; and she had already worried more in those few days than she had in all of her living life with no foreseeable end to it in sight. Things would get far worse before the next five months were up. She could already feel the heat and conflict of it burning in her heart.

It took five months for men to gestate. When that time was over her father wouldn't be Human anymore. In five months time she might only have a gravestone to visit. Or else he'd be an invalid left to linger in a retirement village for the rest of his sorry days. More fantastical, he could be a father again after thirty-eight years, with a brand new alien body and the means and inclination to heap more on top of plenty. How could she face any of those futures? What kind of people would they become in their struggle to survive? Always she was his daughter. She stood beside him through every battle just as he had done for her, but this was more than the sum of them. It wasn't going to be all right. There was no normal for them to return to, just a different reality to embrace.

"Wife." Hyeonsu's smooth voice broke through the haze of her mental flagellation.

"Oh, my swain." She sat up straight in her chair.

"What do you do in here for so long?" He wondered as he entered the room and saw that she hadn't packed her attaché case, but she was sitting at her desk with her coat on.

"Nothing certain. Is dinner prepared?"

"Just only. What has happened, my warrior?"

"Ahh, sire, what should I say?" She hesitated to speak because she didn't want to worry him. She kept his world very small and problem free. Contented men didn't rail, and there were precious few who were as completely gratified as her Hyeonsu; but he was family too, and he deserved to know what was about to draw most of her time away from their happy hearth. "My father…he… good God, you need to know…my sire is caught."

"Caught how?" he questioned innocently.

"Sire anon." Her face flushed bright red.

Hyeonsu stared at her, and for the life of her she couldn't read his paused expression. "By whom?" he asked, and she nearly fainted.

"In the name of my father's God on high, if I knew that I would be sitting in jail right now! If I had e'en an *ounce* of my daddy's spirit I would go raze all of Aldermont City down into this wretched Earth."

"Surely it…." But he didn't finish the sentence. "Anon, come. The ean await."

"Tell them nothing."

"Ne'er to mind it, I shall not." He walked away. "And they will suspect nothing if you can manage to remove your *coat* before you come to the table."

Hyeonsu was a straightforward man, but if he could suddenly guard his words, then things were worst than she thought.

Chapter 6 ─────────────────────

Afternoon.
Hydra Supercluster.
Border of One City.

The *Solace* was a purely functional ship in comparison to other vessels in the Medical Corps fleet. Being small, high-speed, and stocked to the nines were its only selling points. It easily kept up with the TAU Sword and its Valefore escort as they crossed the empty space between the Andromeda galaxy and the Local Edge at hyper speed. They had to be mindful of the busy through lanes and could only use their fold engines after they'd reached the Maduro Void. Even with the added five million light years, they were on the border of One before 6:00 a.m. Universal Time.

Home was a vast stretch of sunless space just outside of Abell 1060 in the Hydra Supercluster. One City stood in no one's orbit. It relied on its own resources and rendered unambiguous aid to all of its allies; but such a plain, uninteresting label could in no way describe the ultra-modern sprawl of the massive network of stationary satellites. It was chosen simply because it translated the same in every known language. The central point, the grand city peopled by nomads who called no planet their own.

Blue and copper solar panels gleamed in the starlight. Each station was unique unto itself. Some had their own growing ecosystem, complete with an artificial sun. Others were picturesque suburban habitats wrapped around rotating towers and aesthetically embellished with domed parks.

Glass hulls offered a glimpse into an ideal society where there was no crime or fear; all of the citizens valued their hard-won independence too much to defile it. Every make, model, creed, code, and species lived side by side completely unconcerned with their differences. In the Nation Fleet there was only one way of life, one heart to protect.

Municipalities were set like sentinels before the centers of government. Eight-lane super-highways kept traffic flowing smoothly through the veins of the tiny cities with separate purposes. West One was the mecca of all things cultural, where the Guild of Artisans held sway. Chief among them was the Hori (tattoo) Guild, their ink was the life's blood of the Nation Fleet. UEDF bases were concentrated in North One around Central Command. The gateway city of South One was a hospitality station that provided everything from free hotels to wholesome entertainment for citizens and visitors alike; but mainly support services for the engineers who spent their lives jockeying from ship to ship with no permanent residence.

Every satellite had a variety of airfields and harbors to accommodate everything from personal landers to the fast-paced network of couriers who made drops and took pickups in a matter of seconds; but they paled beside the breathtaking spacescape of the Star Port.

Artificial gravity wells moored bustling hubs that never fell still. Crafts of all sizes buzzed around the huge open bays of anchored platforms that made battle fortresses look like parked toys alongside of them. In the massive hangars, construction and repair went on thirty-six hours a day, seven days a week with a rotating staff that employed nearly two-thirds of the entire population. The Corps of Engineers maintained the fleet and called the Star Port homebase. Nothing went on, in, or out of those great holds without their supervision.

The *Solace* and her convoy took the fast-moving east skyway to Medical Corps Command, where they landed on the emergency intake airfield of the Main Hospital. East One was a giant laboratory sprinkled generously with classrooms and schoolhouses that fed the mind and kept discovery in the forefront of their society. Ricki welcomed the gentle breeze and the familiar faces that were waiting on the tarmac for them, but Galleon scowled. Up until now everything had gone so smoothly that she had dared to believe that, for once, the dissenting voices had been properly heeled by the strangeness of the situation—if not exactly by the general's orders. She kicked herself for her complacency before she turned on Dr. Ricki. "You called them."

"I assure you, doctor, that I did not." Ricki smiled as she helped to guide Captain Hjorth's cryotube down the ramp and into his frantic wife's arms.

"OH MY GOD!" Ella screamed over and over again as she wiped the frost off of the viewport to lay her naked eyes on the science experiment that was left of her husband. "Is he *dead*?! Aaron! Aaron!"

"Don't be absurd," Galleon scoffed with a roll of her eyes. Dramatic scenes like this was exactly why she chose to focus on laboratory studies over practicing in the field.

"Then why is he in stasis?" Ella's empirical curiosity managed to punch through her grief. "Was it medically necessary? Was he injured?"

"It was my call," Galleon loathed to admit, anticipating another howl of hysteria, "to prevent any further mental contamination."

"W-what?" The vague non-answer made absolutely no sense to Ella.

"It's standard practice in the Yomin Legion. They put all of their patients in stasis during transport to arrest unnecessary disruptive outbursts."

"Let's get him inside." Nanette stepped forward to gently take control of the situation. She could tell by the look on Ella's face that she was within a few more of Dr. Galleon's insensitive words of a disruptive outburst. "It's going to take hours to revive him. In the meantime Parvati had the foresight to schedule a meeting to choose a special team just to handle Aaron's case, which you are more than welcome to sit in on."

That cool, sweet voice, another one of the Master's nonpareil creations. Galleon felt surrounded. From the verenigd of tall, statuesque males climbing out of their Valfores; to the regal dark beauty at her side; and now the tiny tow-haired sprite with the sparkling blue eyes whose presence alone had completely eclipsed her authority — each and every one of them hung like a mirror over her head constantly reflecting all of the flaws of her random birth. She followed quietly with a glance toward the perfect sky, that was every bit as engineered as her escorts, sensing the presence of another Yomin — one significantly more powerful and crafty who had been left to wait a bit too long.

The general warned her to be very careful, but equal, in her distribution of knowledge. To say what needed to be said to everyone who needed to hear it. She'd failed in that aspect of her duty when she left Admiral Jackson Hill in the dark. The other Yomin, for all of their gifts, were still controllable. They didn't react in ways that she couldn't anticipate. Perhaps that was the difference between a clone and born stock.

"All such...*things*... are not created equal."Parvati sighed.

"Did you say something, doctor?" Ricki turned to her.

"Just contemplating the report that I need to make to the General," she covered.

"Yes. Events have taken an unexpected turn."

"They most certainly have."

Midnight.
Earth.
Greeves Airfield.

The winter was slow to release its hold on the Earth, which suited Steven just fine. He was a creature of deep space; the natural environment of any planet was a constant discomfort for him. The weather was never the same. The sun was always too bright and the ground stood unnervingly still underfoot. He felt like a fish out of water, something he'd just have to get used to for the next five months.

In the world according to Steven R. Sunduvall, there were three types of communication: things he needed to hear, things that he didn't want to hear, and the things he let people get away with telling him. An admittedly narrow view, but all a lifelong soldier really needed. He'd gleaned enough from his first husbandry appointment to realize that his temporary grounding was about to be stamped with a very long extension. He didn't want anyone trying to explain to him why—or plead with him over—what was best for him in his condition. The decision was his alone.

With that single thought in mind, he woke up early and drove out to Greeves so that he could work alone in the silence that he thought such a moment deserved.

The UEDF had no shortage of Valefore fighter jets, but there were only a handful of customized ones that everyone recognized—including their enemies. War machines like *Kingdom Come* and *Glory Hallelujah* were as infamous as their verenigd pilots. *Valnir*, with her bright paint job and a technical genius at her helm, drove many—fazed and foxed—to their ready deaths. The *Witch's Hammer* set raiders scurrying for cover with only the glint of starshine off of her fiery red hull. The Grey Ghost piloted a sleek, modish camouflaged Valefore called the *Wraith* because no one ever saw it coming until it was far too late. Then there were ones like the silvery-white *Sixpence* that needed no introduction. Steven walked past the *Weep for Me* and thought how she'd be the only all-black Valefore in service after today. Intricate reliefs of ancient battles were etched in metallic onyx on both sides of her ebony hull. It matched in pure fury the enigma of her pilot, who had racked up more confirmed kills in single combat than anyone else in the UEDF.

Just beyond her nose sat *Hells Deep*, aptly named and emblazoned with the jolly roger skull and crossed bones from their ancient origins on Earth.

Like a flag hoisted over a battlefield, she stood for something beyond the sum of her parts. She was meant to outlive the pilot. She'd already served twenty-three masters since the conception of the UEDF, and Steven held the honor the longest. The undisputed best piloting the best, it was a throne he had relished—humbly so—for over forty years. It was absolutely impossible for him to fathom that this could be the last time he'd ever see her whole while she was still his. Life was a funny thing, full of surprises and the next horizon to cross; he just never imagined that he wouldn't be doing that in his Valefore.

Packaging the jet for storage went much faster than he'd hoped. He dropped *Hells Deep*'s engine and disconnected her jump drive. He folded the wings and set the onboard computer into a dormant cycle. He sat in the cockpit until the residual harmonic echo faded. He leaned back to take in the moment, trying to gain some prospective that would ease *Hells*' passing but there was nothing beyond the deafening silence, and nothing could make this right except the day he turned her back on.

Morning.
Centaurs Wall.
The *Southerland*.

"Baby girl, I'm callin' you!" Jackson raised his voice.

"Coming!" Lee sang back.

"Then come now!" he bayed impatiently as he waited on the couch with a comb in one hand, the duty roster in the other, and a cigarette tucked into the corner of his lips. He had a million and one things to do today, not including preparing his young daughter for school on the *Lethe* where she would take the flight exam and study English in classrooms full of other frisky cadets, just like her. He expected that she would return still completely unable to put two understandable words together in the old tongue, though she'd be a fully-licensed pilot ready to move on to large-vessel training.

A skinny, knobby-kneed, little stick of a kid at the bare end of her tweenie feralness came bouncing out of the door at the end of the hall. She circled the room once before plopping down on the floor in front of her father to have her wild shock of red hair tamed.

"Keep still." Jackson took one last long drag before putting out his cigarette. He'd need both his hands—and probably a leg lock—to hold his girl-child down long enough to braid her hair. "Don't give nobody a hard time, savvy me?" He reiterated a few last-minute rules.

"Yes, Pa." Lee nodded in ready agreement.

"Study ya books and mind Miss Ne Ne. I don't wanna hear nothin' 'bout no foolishness. An' if you're brass enough to get into a fight, I'm gonna be waitin' for you with the right attitude ta tan that narrow hide, ya hear me?"

"Yes, Pa." She giggled, which wasn't the reaction he was aiming for.

"Go easy on these braids so they can last you. Nobody's gonna be around to scratch out ya head. Didja pack your sleeping bonnet?"

"I do not like my sleeping bonnet."

"I didn't ask you if you liked it, just make sure you pack it." The doorbell's chime interrupted what was about to blossom into a full-on bag check.

"I will get it!" Lee sprung to her feet and pressed the *door open* button leaving Jackson with bare seconds left to hastily cover head or else be completly exposed to the person he'd been expecting.

"Good morrow." A tall blonde goddess of a warrior smiled down at the young girl who stood in her shadow.

"Good morrow!" Lee returned with an ear-to-ear grin.

"Admiral, on't the morrow." Miss Ne Ne was as formal with her commanding officer as the day that she'd first met him, despite having played an active roll in helping to raise young Lee.

"Warrior glao," Jackson returned the formality in his politest Of Megt while he adjusted the straw Stetson he wore in lieu of a kuffiya. His aversion to draping ran deep enough for him to find fault in the simple everyday head covering that was readily worn by all men—of megt and non-megt—when etiquette called for it. "You are right on time."

"I trust that everything is in order and that you are ready to go." Miss Ne Ne tweaked the girl's chin.

"Yea verily." Lee confirmed.

"Then fetch out your bags." She sent Lee on her way. "Off you go."

"Thanks for this." Jackson blushed a little.

"There is no need." Miss Ne Ne wouldn't hear of it. "Lee's education cannot be asided, and there is what business to attend to in Virginia Bay on behald of the Council of Warriors. It is a fact that the old general will soon step down. There has been much debate over who will succeed him. I heard a rumor that Management thinks that there should be a vote."

"Yeah, I wish 'em luck." He snickered. "There's no way that any UEDF matter will ever be up for the vote again."

"I happen to most wholeheartedly agree with you. That is why I will try to dissuade the council round before it goes any further. Just the mere ideation that civilian administration—or worse, the Ministry of cultural affairs—will try to interfere in UEDF business is enough to distract the entire Ready Line."

Jackson wondered about the temperament of the Ready Line front. He wasn't the point in charge. That was Admiral Seong Oh Jun's jurisdiction. No one could be less involved with the plight of the warriors left to die by the score in a forgotten corner of space fighting the last hours of the Demon War than Admiral Seong. And if there was anyone supporting the civilian's intrusion into military affairs it was also Admiral Seong. Jackson was about to ask Miss Ne Ne some very hard to answer questions, instead he let his daughter's loud shuffling distract him. Though he was loathed to admit it, certain things had to remain unsaid until the old general stepped down.

"All set!" Lee came bounding back with her duffel bag slung over her shoulder.

"C'mere, girlie." Jackson hugged her tight. "Yeah."

"Paaaaa," she groaned.

"I know I'm embarrassin' you but you're my one piece. You don't get to leave my sight without a snuggle."

"I love you, Pa."

"I love you, baby." He walked her out. "Be good." He strengthened his voice to deliver one last sound warning.

"I will." Lee waved as she stepped onto the moving walkway behind Miss Ne Ne.

Jackson swallowed, already missing his dear child. An entire school semester without her was going to be rough, but there were things that he could only accomplish with her safely out of ear-and-eyeshot. He didn't want to worry her unnecessarily or expose her to certain conditions that came with being a mature Yomin.

He waited until Lee was out of sight before he turned back inside to answer the insistent ringing of the incoming call alert that had been trying to disrupt his fond farewell ever since Lee came whirling out of her room.

"There you are," Tracy grumbled. It was barely 7:00a.m. but already his pale green eyes were blazing with annoyance. Jackson cringed for the poor souls under Tracy's command who were sure to be ribbed, reamed, and ridden en masse today. "I knew you hadn't gone on duty yet."

"I was seein' my Lee off, if you don't mind me takin' a personal minute."

"I sure do when I gotta deal with the pot you done stirred."

"How you figure?" Jackson decided to get as much information out of Tracy as he could before their conversation deteriorated into the typical bickering just before they called Fran in to referee.

"Don't even, dude! Pia rang me." Tracy growled.

"*Pia*? What's she got to do with the price of bread?"

"She spun an interestin' yarn 'bout how Beau suddenly needed some robing in the middle of his shift."

"So?"

"How far are you gonna take this? 'Til I hop in *my* plane an' come ta smack ya chops?" Tracy didn't mind leveling crude threats. Jackson didn't mind it either, especially when it helped to drive the point home in a way that only long-time confidants could appreciate. "What the Human's Hell are you doin'? Don't you know that the General *hates* you?! Still you go meddlin' in his business."

"The General doesn't hate me per se."

"You're a thorn in his side, an' you're too high up on the food chain for him to ignore considerin' how he intends to hand pick his successor."

"Lettin' Aaron disappear into Corps Command wasn't an option." With his tone alone, Jackson made it very clear that certain aspects of recent events were not up for debate. "We have the responsibility to help him and to find out exactly what happened."

"The General doesn't think so."

"Well that's not good enough this time."

"Look, I get you. I think it sucks too. That damn Galleon thought she was doin' somethin' when she left you out of the loop. I tried to tell her."

"So there was a meeting." Jackson felt vindicated. He knew in his bones that there were forces at work behind his back. There was no reason for a point admiral to be left out of a conversation that had anything to do with issues under his jurisdiction, most especially ones that directly concerned the loss of his personnel. While another point admiral, who had nothing at all to do with any of the recent events, was sitting in as if the two of them were interchangeable.

"She called a remote tête-à-tête while the *Solace* was en route to One." Tracy scratched behind his ear—his subconscious *tell* when he was about to line up an exact chain of events. "I questioned why you weren't included, and she had somethin' snide ta say—Elders love her 'cause I sure don't. That's what started me keepin' my ears up, waitin' for your move. Sure enough, Pia called me full to burstin'. After all the years she's been married ta Beau she still can't tell from what.

"There was another meetin' this mornin'. Galleon reported that Ella showed up at Corps Command ahead of the *Solace*. I didn't have to wonder how that happened for a minute, now did I?"

"I'm sure she wasn't gonna tell Ella. So what lie was gonna get stuffed into that hole?" Jackson left it up to Tracy to conclude for himself.

"You've gotta keep your eye on the big picture. This isn't the time to cross swords with the General. We've all got too much to lose. I've got reason to believe that Fran doesn't know about any of this. There's not a damn thing we can do for Aaron right now, but everybody needs to know about the new fucked-up mandate that came about because of him."

Jackson checked his watch—already ahead of Tracy—while he waited for the Deep Space Network to connect his call. "It's around 3:00 a.m. the day before yesterday on Earth now. So Fran should be up an' about since he's on Universal Time; but, I dunno if the Earth's in a good position to receive a live-call."

"Use the LOC, I ain't got all day." Tracy sucked his impatience through his teeth. "I dunno why there's such a yen for that lump of charcoal in the ass-crack of space what don't got no room for aliens no how.

"Just watch, the whole rest of the Horde's gonna get their heads bashed in by them Neanderthals down there. We're gonna be the only ones left, an' how's that gonna work out? The few women in our ranks ain't got nothin' for us, an' all our kids are swingin' monkeys."

"Pata!" Tracy's teenaged son, Shannon, protested from the background as he strolled through the common area at just the right moment to overhear.

"Yeah, I'm talkin' about you! Go study a book instead of prunin' yaself like a goddamned houseplant waitin' around for some warrior ta take you indoors!"

Jackson smiled at the comedy, feeling rather comforted that he had a daughter instead of a son. There were far fewer choices for a warrior. She had to *become*, she could never just *be*.

"I'm gonna *have* your gena later, bet! Ain't nobody sleepin' in this joint tonight!" Tracy turned back to the monitor still foaming at the mouth.

He raked the kuffiya off his head as if he were upset that he had put it on while he sat in the privacy of his own home. The Kazen male was a proud UEDF lifer; but he was also willed to a Pannarian warrior, and sometimes those two roles fell into conflict. "This is the third son for me that devious witch done sold off. What the Human's Hell does she think, I'm pullin' 'em out of a hat?! She donno how fast I can find another place for me an' mine to be. Did that call connect yet?!"

"No, sir." Jackson was just able to hold in his laughter as he gave up on the standard video omnidirectional communication channel in favor of the long-range video feed that Tracy suggested.

"Didn't I say ta use LOC?! Everybody must want some of Tracy today!"

"Yaw, sir. Sorry, sir."

"And here I thought that Fran was gonna see us civil for once."

Chapter 7 —————————————————

Afternoon.
Earth.
Solito Lake Retirement Village.

Nothing compared to the smell of fresh-cut grass.
The beautiful lawns of Solito Lake were a true indulgence
on a planet that couldn't sustain even a blade of real grass
in an unregulated environment. It would be very difficult
for earthlings to believe that people would trample on
such precious plants for the sake of a game, but golf was
practically a national pastime in the Nation Fleet, one
of the only occasions where a spacefaring people could
actually touch a genuine growing thing. The breathtaking
landscape that surrounded the village was the height of
opulence. No feature was overlooked—from the golden
sparkling lake, to the pristine gardens of cultivated
flowers—and the residents were sweetly grateful for
every spectacular acre.

A rare day off was eagerly spent on the luscious golf
course. Steven and Barry lagged behind their friends in a
cart of their own as they crossed the open field between

the fourth and fifth holes. They could hear the echoing laughter that rang out after each completed joke, their silence better suited the seriousness of their mood.

"Why'd you miss the morning brief?" Barry asked. "I know you were out at Greeves before us because *Hells Deep* was packed away."

"I needed some space," Steven admitted quietly.

"You've got the worst timing. You really should've heard what was said firsthand. Apparently there's a new rule of the day. Any construct—Veddified POW, Changeling, whatever else—has gotta be cleared for duty through a new evaluation called a P-20. No exceptions."

"That's just a ploy to knock Jake out of the running for the big chair." Steven brushed off what he interpreted as the latest line of a growing laundry list of excuses to eliminate fair candidates from consideration for the soon-to-be-vacated position of Supreme Command General.

"It's gonna affect you too if you fall subject to the Human League's laws. Worst still, Dr. Galleon's got *carte blanche* to lock folks up for crazy with that P-20. Ezzie's gonna escort Jake in, so I doubt Galleon'll fuck with him; but she's already made one kill. It would make the General's whole damn year if she could snag you on a psych hold. We gotta come clean to Fran. There's no point keepin' quiet what your waistline won't be able to in a few weeks."

"Women don't go blabbing their business too early."

"Are you a woman now?"

Steven slammed on the breaks purposefully, and Barry went tumbling out to the entertainment of the other guys.

"Ha! What happened?" Dustin teased. "Is the honeymoon over so soon?" He was a jovial prankster in his own special way so he could really enjoy a good pratfall. He helped Barry to his feet while he laughed in his face.

"Why's every game gotta to turn into a jackass parade?" Jacob scolded, much less amused. He'd been an increasingly moody mess for weeks; and all the reason why they opted for driving golf carts instead of taking their usual carefree stroll across the fairway as they navigated the course. He raked his wet grey hair out of his face, having sweat much more profusely than the relatively small amount of exercise that they'd had so far would call for. The genetic cloak Jacob wore was failing against the resurgence of the Yomin biology that had been forced into his veins long ago. No one would make mention; it wasn't the place of age-old friends. Their commitment demanded much more than empty commentary. "Foolishness is half the reason why people hate us like they hate the Devil." He carried on, getting more irritated by the minute.

"So what did the Hand have to say?" Fran asked as something of an afterthought while he staked his ball. "Didn't Sunny finally bring 'em by?"

"Are we playing or gossiping?" Steven sighed flatly.

"That bad, huh?" Fran took a mighty swing that launched his ball well across the bunker and into range of the sixth hole. He expected more out of his well-aimed ball than he did from the report of Steven's doctor's appointment.

"Are you okay?" Dustin asked.

Steven held his tongue. In all fairness, Dustin hadn't been on-world for their recent shenanigans. He didn't know about the brewing question that was hanging overhead, so snapping at him for his public display of concern would only start a fight.

"Not unless breeding at his age is fatal." Barry came right out with it, to everyone's horror. Steven, who had just leaned over to set his ball, nearly did a forward flip to rival Barry's when those stark naked words rang out.

"For real?!" Jacob's voice went up two octaves. "How'z that even possible? You're friggin' old as dirt!"

"Dude!" Dustin scowled. "Who was drinkin' too much of what when *that* happened?"

"I told you jackanapes not to fuck around in the valley!" Fran shook his head, exasperated and chock-full of righteous indignation. Their excursions had always been on his radar to put a stop to, but there was something whimsical about older Humans that he'd—regrettably—mistaken as benign. He'd speak on it, joke about it, rail a bit when he felt like getting rowdy over nothing. Whatever precaution he did attempt was only a formality that had just blown up in his face like a land mine. "Why didn't you use the implants I gave you?!"

"Because!" Steven felt obliged to bristle at the authoritative tone.

"Because why?!" Fran pressed.

Which only made Steven more defiant. He squared his shoulders at the man who stood head, shoulders, and chest over him ready to return every bit of the fire he'd received. "The only manual birth control invented for men since Julius Caesar slipped on a sheepskin is a Goddamned bondage, sadomasochistic torture devise! I'm not runnin' nothin' up nowhere unnatural!"

"But you'll let a warrior ride you bareback?!"

"She wasn't a warrior." Barry tried to clarify things a bit.

"Don't go pickin' nits after one of you old bastards have been caught naked from the waist down!" Fran refused to digest excuses. "I've said it an' said it! I should've broke ya damned legs before I let y'all rogue outta here stupid an' slink back mangy!"

"Yeah, that's enough yowlin' 'bout the place," Jacob intervened. "You've had your good, long say. Now unless you're gonna kick the not-yet outta him, an' save us all a heap of trouble, don't make no more of it."

"How'd Sunny bear up? That's what I wanna know." Dustin shrugged. "I bet she took to her bed with the shock. And what the hell is goin' through your head right now? We saw what you did to *Hells Deep*. There are no airlocks to throw yourself out of down here, ya know. An' we'll let Galleon hole you up for crazy before we find you stretched out in your dress uniform."

"I'm not upset over what happened, it's the consequences I'm struggling with…and the way Sunny looked at me…I dunno," Steven confessed. His mind flashed back to the previous night as he sat at his kitchen counter trying not to be sick while his life became a case study. "I don't know how I feel."

"It's called shame," Jacob offered dryly.

"Gee, thanks, guys. Don't go killing me with compassion." Steven retreated to his old fail-safe of sarcasm to keep from clubbing someone over the head with his driver.

"You'd be nicer to women on the whole if you wanted somebody to coddle you. This is the best that a set of longtime fools can manage on such short notice." Barry was always able to find the calm center of even the worst catastrophe. Years of reaping the bitter fruit of his own mistakes had given him the ability and the patience to roll with life's punches. His sobriety was infectious. Soon enough everyone, including Fran, was nodding in ready agreement. "The thing to do now is prepare, most especially after what Jackie and Tracy had to say, and considering how the Human League sets the bar on Earth.

They'll be comin' for their due. They're gonna make you pay for this with your humanity if you stay here."

Steven breathed a hard, frustrated sigh. "Where can I go considering how the General has me by the balls? If I'm not under the Horde's banner *literally*, then I've gotta serve out my probation on the Ready Line, where the only health care is a stick to bite down on." Steven was very frank with things that they all tried not to remember so clearly, such as the event that led to him serving eight years before the mast of the Two Stones work camp for murder, and the terrible deal that his brothers-in-arms struck with the general on his behalf that effectively exiled the three biggest threats to his absolute control of the UEDF to the most remote, inhospitable corner of their territory.

"We'll survive the General's rule," Jacob spoke with confidence.

"Maybe you will, but I'm at the end of the line." Steven wasn't ready to be placated. "I tried to listen with understanding while Sunny was talking things over with the Hand, but none of it made sense. Expansion. Scrambling. The Human League's laws, what the fuck? So be it. We've all got to give way at some point. I guess this is just my time."

"B's right." Fran sighed in complete acceptance and without any hard feelings. "You're not sick ta die. Good medicine'll see you clear, an' the Hand's renowned for their doctoring. You're in the best place you can be. There's a whole hospital dedicated to Paternal Science, plus an alien agency set up to advocate for ya rights. There's perks to bein' downed on a world where everybody and their half-wit kin gets a say. Even if you're scrambled it's no never mind. It's Horde business handled within our doors. All we've gotta do is keep quiet 'til the General retires. You can't get jammed up if nobody knows about what happened to you."

"That would work if we didn't live surrounded by the nosiest bitches God ever gave breath to," Dustin reminded them.

"Man, listen." Jacob waved off even the notion of such a small problem. "If there's anythin' we know how to do it's drive people to distraction."

Chapter 8 ————————————————————

Morning.
One City.
Medical Corps Main Hospital.

"You're wrong about this, Parvati! Just as you're wrong about *most* of the things you choose not to fully investigate!" Nanette roared behind Dr. Galleon as she chased her from room to room of the pharmaceutical refrigerator. It was inevitable. The patient had to be revived and questioned. But the odd, nearly counterproductive tactics that were being wielded against an obviously confused patient left a bad taste in Nanette's mouth. "Captain Hjorth needs to be under Cana's care. This line of misdirection will only collapse him. The Intel he could give us will be lost!"

"Cana is just a Muse." Galleon knew she was in for a fight. She expected to have to defend every action she took and every word she spoke. Her decisions would be questioned, and her reports would be combed through by everyone from here to the Ready Line. Having to contend with her most outspoken rival was only the opening volley.

Dr. Nanette Crash had a whole lot to say for someone who was officially on vacation. Galleon began to suspect that Nanette had no intentions of leaving One and that she would use her rank to bully her way onto the case permanently. These were the most critical hours; Galleon had to take in silent stride whatever her colleague had to say so long as Nanette left One City with Dr. Ricki as planned.

"Cana's a *Melete* High Muse. Regulation is her job." Nanette was well aware of the fact that her words had been falling on deaf ears since Aaron Hjorth's assessment, but they bore saying anyway. If something so profound ever happened to her she would want someone to fight for her, even if they were ultimately unsuccessful. It was too late to divulge concerns once everything was said and done, the way people tended to do to make themselves feel better after having stood idle.

"It's the primary function of her caste. That doesn't make her an expert." Galleon was less than receptive. She'd heard it all over and over again until the words lost their meaning. She was very sure that nothing would sway her, though it was tempting to let Captain Hjorth and his problematic case disappear into the Yomin hive that a certain Mistress Cana had founded in the heart of the Nation Fleet. But if that were part of the general's design he wouldn't have given her command.

"Yes, it does!" Nanette slammed the door closed before Galleon could escape again. "You have to do what's best for your patient. Treating him like a Human psych case isn't what's best. He's a Yomin construct now."

"The fact of which I am well aware of."

"Then why are you holding him on a P-20?!"

"As a consequence of genetic tampering, all Changelings are unbalanced."

"If they're uncasted!"

"So instead of providing proper medical care, he should be turned into a slave of some long-dead masters, just as you once were?" Parvati tried to distract Nanette by hitting her where it would hurt. The Yomin, most especially, didn't like being reminded from whence they sprang, which she often used as a weapon. "How could we ever be sure that the information Cana extracted from him was accurate? I can't report undocumented holistic treatments as fact. I don't know why I'm wasting my breath on a leftover?"

Nanette didn't bite, but her eyes were beginning to spark like the tip of a lit fuse. "It's nothing to be ashamed of. Everybody strives to be something in life. The Yomin have the advantage of having a direction programmed into our genes. We don't have to follow it. Just having it creates a sense of purpose. Without it we're every bit as lost as you people are."

"You're simplifying a serious medical issue."

"And you're practicing junk science!"

"The General put me in charge! If you've got a problem with that, then take it up with him, if you dare."

"The only reason you're in charge is because you won't ask any questions. I rue the day that the Medical Corps became militarized. More and more doctors are putting their oath to serve the interest of the UEDF ahead of their oath to do no harm. You'll sweep everything away, the General will get to walk out of the door with a clean slate, but where will that leave Aaron? Or should I just call him *Subject Zero* and get it over with?"

"How dare you…"

"Please, Parvati. It's just you and I here."

"There is no conspiracy. There are no unseen enemies lurking in the shadows. The Crazy Eights were victims of *normal* circumstances: namely the various groups of raiders who have been stealing from us and ambushing our small convoys for years. If you want to petition the General, go ask him why he doesn't do something about those bunch of scavenging barbarians?"

"Transfer Arron to the *Southerland*. He needs to be in Cana's care." Nanette repeated her simple point.

"No."

"His wife is a doctor, too. She won't stand for this."

"She'll do what I tell her is best for him." Dr. Galleon opened the door very slowly, smiling. "You could set off a firestorm and probably win the day, but you won't. You've always been a big-picture thinker—a real credit to your species…or, rather, the ingenuity of your masters."

Nanette put her equal on the floor with a knelling slap. The niceties were over. Now there was nothing left but hard feelings and open warfare. "Who the fuck are you taking to? Huh?! I'm flesh and blood, and just as alive as you are; and you'll show me some *respect,* or you'd better be ready to prove your point with your bare hands!"

"Nan!" Ricki ran in just in time to stop Nanette from taking another swing.

"Are you really afraid of this single-cell organism? Look at her!" Nanette tried to shake some sense into Ricki. "Just another damned fool cloaked in threats and arrogance!" She whirled around to have at Dr. Galleon again, setting off another round of wrestling between herself and Ricki. "Turn Aaron's care over to Cana! Do the right thing for once in your miserable life!"

"Is this all we're capable of?" Ricki had to stand between the two women to keep the peace. "Can't we disagree without coming to blows? Why don't we just admit that we don't know what to do for Captain Hjorth? We have no idea how it even happened. Let's start with that, follow procedure, and keep an open mind. All this arguing is just wasting precious time and not accomplishing anything." Ricki's cool logic was hard to deny. Half of their frustration stemmed from not knowing what to do, or how to remain in compliance with the general's guidelines. Tied hands could not accomplish much. "This won't go any further unless you push it. Will it, Dr. Galleon?"

"…No." Galleon nursed her split lip. "We passed the usual words as far as I'm concerned. This isn't the first time we've come to blows, and I'm sure it won't be the last. Enjoy your leave, Dr. Crash. Preferably out of my sight."

"I can see that I'm going to serve time for your murder one of these days." Nannette stomped off.

"Nan." Ricki tried to stop her from leaving the conversation on such a bitter note.

"Let her go." Galleon eased into a seat. "And please don't consult with her on the Hjorth case. It's none of her business, unless all of you Yomin think that everything to do with any one of you is all of your business."

"Don't worry about me. I didn't volunteer to be on the team for a reason. I can't, in good conscience."

"Your survival instincts are second to none. I don't blame you for keeping your head down. That's exactly what I'm trying to do in my own way. Captain Hjorth's future isn't the only one at stake."

Whip and Wether

Chapter 9 ———————————————

Evening.
Earth.
Foundation Hill Men's Hospital.

"We have thought on't," Mect started the presentation to Sunduvall. "The common scrambler used today is a sub-demi cocktail with nonracial specific architecture, very much like the Core's POW patriotism process. It is favored for its simplicity and neutrality. The recipient becomes something that is recognized as an entirely new species called the *Endamnu*—a rather mean and uncreative turn of words meant to brand without an iron." All of them knew the truth of that far too well. Doctors had become pawns of the Human League, meting out their brand of justice one patient at a time.

Mect continued, "It is a single-dose process, injected and fast-acting in persons who are otherwise healthy. If an ailment is detected, the scrambler is suspended and has only a baseline effect.

"What concerned us, apart from your good sire's genome, is the scrambler's high fetal-morbidity rate.

Forty-eight percent slip the quick when the scrambler is administered under the five-week mark. Sire Sunduvall is already at considerable risk. The law says that he must be scrambled, but why be scrambled if it is likely to kill him or the cause for it?"

"And if we were to wait beyond the point of danger?" Sunduvall asked just to confirm her knowledge.

"Unfortunately, your sire is set to break in," Vladimir cited. "While the law allows for a grace period, we fear that your sire's body will not, and he is far too fragile to come through that in good shape. So what we have devised is a way to scramble him over the course of three stages."

"Aye," Mect agreed. "Instead of the standard mix we will use a version of the old Master I scrambler. It is species-specific with distinct advantages. The Yomin are strong breeders. Even at full strength their genetic resequencers never caused anyone to slip, but the effect is more immediate. Unlike the sub-demi scrambler, the Master I will run its full course, even in an unhealthy patient. That is the reason for the stages. Sire Sunduvall will be sturdier in crisis, as the Yomin heal very quickly. Retarded aging and a dynamic regenerative system is a by-product, but he will not have the vigorous immunity to viruses that he did as a Human. The antibodies in his blood now are the only ones he will ever have. If he has never had a cold he must be infected and allowed to process it naturally before he is scrambled, or else he will have no defenses against it in the future."

"He has had several colds since moving on-world." Sunduvall heaved a grateful sigh.

What the Humans thought of lightly as a common illness was the number-one killer of aliens; most especially the Yomin, who tended to have more regular and personal contact with Humans. It was the only reason their mortality rates were so high here on Earth.

Every year there were long lines at the Foundation's clinics to receive the new stype, which had to be administered within ten hours of infection, or death was imminent. For a man like her father who was used to being sick from time to time as a Human, and with his nearly complete aversion to doctors, it wouldn't be a stretch to find him dead of a spring cold. She had to actively put aside the urge to infect him one last time just for good measure.

Her shuffling thoughts had managed to block out the rest of the selling points, leaving her to wonder what she had missed but too embarrassed to ask. Though she did have one very important point to bring up. "As a Master I he will fall to the Season as the Yomin do."

"The Season will take him," Mect confirmed. " Dare I say, he will much resemble the local glasses. He could be classified and casted, but that would make him a Master II."

"I would prefer that he be assigned to a caste from the start," Sunduvall said without hesitation. "It would only be harder on him later; in fact he might not agree to it at all, if it is put to him as a choice. I know my father well. He needs a caste to stay in healthful function or else he will wholly succumb to his demons." Her own words sent an uncomfortable chill crawling down her spine, and a scary replay of the highlights from her hellish week came racing back to her conscious mind. Her breath shortened with the mere ideation of the havoc her dear father would wreak if he were left as an unclassified Yomin.

"Which one did you have in mind?" Tendart asked outright, blocking her full slip into the waking dream that so often kept her prisoner these days. He had no argument to lend to their conversation after having met the man and holding him in ready account. He could imagine the kind of misery Sire Sunduvall would court until every bit of his warrior's house laid in ruin, if he were left to linger wild and undeclared.

"If it were really my choice, he would be a scholar or an engineer," Sunduvall said. He possesses both genius-level intelligence and the applicable skill to make a successful transition, but he is a fighter first and foremost. He would always suffer the loss if I took that away from him." Sunduvall read over the formula on paper and signed off on her request. Their next appointment would be her father's last day as a Human. Something about that realization made her very sad, but one final point of interest cut her doldrums short. "Curious, I see that this scrambler has a type-four delivery mode, which is very irritating to the Human gastric system."

"We have found that Humans often miscalculate when and how much they have eaten before a procedure," Mect explained. "Anything still digesting could be an unknown factor. The type-four mode is a fail-safe to be most certain that the scrambler is working alone. And in case he is allergic to it in any way, it can be neutralized before too much is absorbed." She fully concurred with the clever idea. "But only the first dose will be...*colorful*. He will not be Human enough to be affected by the subsequent stages."

Morning.
Earth.
Solito Lake Retirement Village.

Steven lingered in the shower, remembering how good he had felt just six months past after his second wife died. He wasn't really the marrying type—though he had outlived two wives. His second one was a clingy, needy woman who was every bit as destructive toward him as his first.

She loathed his friends and didn't allow them to come over. She was afraid of his grown daughter, so he spent the weekends over at Sunduvall's house just to be able to see her regularly. She hated his career and begged him to retire. Every time he came home from duty she'd bombard him with her mournful, endless nagging. Then—like the garnish on top of all their discord—she was a vengeful woman who meant to have her way. Anything he felt for her soured long before she told out-right lies in a letterwriting campaign to the UEDF Board while he was imprisoned. The only things that stood between him and a dishonorable discharge was the loyal voices of the people he'd served with, and Fran. He didn't leave her after his release. The best place for an enemy was in plain sight; and, being perfectly honest, his last stint in the Two Stones work camp had finally driven the point home—he was never going to have his way by force. He had to learn the fine art of patience.

It only took eighteen months of faithful practice before she finally fretted herself into an early grave and he breathed a very satisfied sigh of relief. He was free, though he wished that he wasn't as glad as he was that she was gone. That seemed like something he'd have to answer for one day if he didn't change his heart.

Every memory of her was a hard and bitter pip. He remembered how he had stared at her coffin feeling nothing but relief. He knew he'd never call her name again in life, or allow anyone to call her name to him. The best way to vanquish an enemy was to forget them. Now he was staring at his own proverbial coffin, and that shrill voice he thought he'd heard days ago returned to mock him. This time it was laughing.

"What's that?" Steven questioned the tiny paper cup that was presented to him.

"Stage One. Drink it." Tendart passed him only what words were necessary.

"And this is supposed to *turn* me?" He chuckled with skepticism. "A few teaspoons of liquid in a shot cup?"

"It will."

"How?" Steven knew he had to press for an explanation. Of Megt was an abrupt tongue. Muted—when spoken calmly—and perfect for all occasions of politesse. There was no room for drawn-out elaborations in a proper man's speech.

"During the first stage the changes will be more internal than external. Any deterioration will be addressed and your genetic markers will be erased leaving your blood centrifuged pure." When Tendart spoke again it was in a more clinical fashion—the only way to disseminate an abundance of information without embarrassing himself.

"Centrifuged? Doesn't that involve spinning?"

"…I suppose that it does." Tendart smiled honestly as he weighed the description against the process he was familiar with, which made Steven nervous.

Steven stared at the colorless medicine with the strange metallic odor, thinking absolutely nothing at all. He had no last words, nor even a witty epitaph to offer at the close of his Human life. "Bottoms up." He took a bold swig as if he were knocking back a whiskey straight, but the liquid absorbed into the flesh of his mouth leaving nothing at all to swallow. "Say, that went down easy."

"Glao." Tendart reached for the empty basin he'd prepared before hand. "Sit down."

"Okay." Steven eased down at the foot of the bed, duly puzzled.

Vladimir entered carrying a bowl of water and a compress cloth. Steven grinned. It was still strange for him to see Micromales who had gentle occupations. In the Nation Fleet, of megt men were quite content to do one of two things without exception—either follow their code, or join the Tactical Armored Division. He'd never seen one become a doctor. They were husbands or soldiers; or soldiers until they became husbands, as if there were no other choices for them in life. Lord Vahe's ranks were filled with white-sheathed virgins just waiting for a warrior to come along and drag them indoors where they'd raise the next generation of vestal brutes—probably with the help of a Dog Brother or two. Life on Earth was truly different if such men could wander out alone rendering benevolent aid in spite of the danger and the uncertainty of a vast multi-species population with no true ties to one another. Steven gulped, trying to rein in his thoughts long enough to access the funny pooling of saliva in his mouth. He swallowed again, too modest to spit out so much in front of an audience, and a bit concerned that more than just spit would come out if he tried.

"Be sick if you must," Tendart encouraged.

"Naaw, I'm good," Steven lied, and what a lie it turned out to be. He was more than merely sick, he was hacking out his back teeth. He began to wonder why one of his lungs wasn't floating in the technicolor mess in the bowl he was clutching.

Stomach acid was a rude, unwelcomed thing. It burned his throat and gums, leaving a sharp, rank taste behind. Soon there was nothing left but the lining and that, too, seemed poised to make a very nasty debut.

Now, Steven had been physically sick before—excess drinking; during enviornmental acclimation—but the very worst part to him was the misery of the dry heave. Everything that could come out had, but the gagging continued until his vision began to tunnel and he hoped that he'd pass out just for some relief. He was reaching that point when a swelling heat took over and fresh misery blossomed for him. He feared it and he screamed without shame or temperament. Steven just screamed.

"Barry!" Aggie trumpeted for her husband as she threw open the front door. She'd been in her garden collecting specimens to take into the lab when it became impossible to ignore the distressing sounds that echoed out of the house next door.

She didn't care at all for Steven Sunduvall, or whatever end he was meeting begging on his knees; though it did strike her as odd that her husband, who was one of his closest companions, seemed set to leave him to his fate. They didn't lock their doors before bedtime to guard against moments like this. The Horde was family, and like a family they looked after one another. But now there were strangers visiting Steven at all hours. His driveway was clogged with tricked-out little sports cars, that belonged to fully sheathed and draped Micromales that no one, save for Sunduvall, knew and she wasn't offering up any explanations. If Steven was dying, then it was happening right now. Aggie had never heard such wrenching illness, not even when she was a practicing medical doctor. It was more than enough to draw her attention—and elevate her hopes—so how could her husband lay comfortably asleep in his bed only yards away from the desperate knell of Steven's last roll around fight with the Devil? She'd have to live with the consequences if Barry missed his final breaths, and that was the only reason she felt obligated to wake him. She would ignore the funny feeling that tugged at her gut just long enough to get the word out. Whatever happened after that could not be blamed on her.

"Barry, are you seriously asleep?" Aggie squared off, arms akimbo, at the sight of the lump in the bed that hadn't been disturbed at all by her alarm. She knew that Barry was a hard sleeper, but this was bordering on the ridiculous.

"I was, yeah." He rolled over, still not ready to wake up.

"Don't you hear that?!" She directed his attention to the howl that was riding on the wind. "Just so you can't say that you didn't know, that's Steven meeting his maker without a shred of dignity. Shouldn't you be there sending haka-prayers on ahead or something?"

"…Sunduvall's got the situation handled."

That funny feeling she'd set aside became a full-blown suspicion. "So you're *not* going to call the others? From the very day that I met any of you, if so much as one of you stubbed your toe the others were right there to kiss it better."

"Steven's been sick lately—not to die sick—just the usual, but you know how he is. Sunny just got tired of trying to run him down to treat him. We're lettin' her handle him how she sees fit."

"Since when?" Aggie challenged Barry's explaination.

"Since when what?"

"Something's voodoo, I see it clearly now. Where is Fran?"

"Why?"

"Because Steven is dying, and you've, obviously, gone mad with grief!"

"Sunduvall's got it." Barry reiterated.

"If you say that again I'm going to go next door myself." Aggie flipped her delicate blonde curls over her shoulder and fixed the most icy, blue-eyed stare she had ever produced on him, and he knew that she wasn't going to back down quietly.

"Sunny's serious about how she wants things. You see she's brought in consultants. We're giving her space, not full lee. Steven's not in any danger. If he was, you know how different things would be right now. So just let the girl-ean have her one day. When she's got the results in her own hands to believe, then we'll close ranks. See?" Barry pointed out the return of the peace when everything fell silent. "He's past the worst of it."

"Since you seem to know, I'm all too willing to leave you with yours, but I honestly didn't think you guys had it in you." Aggie left the room reluctantly.

Barry waited until he heard the front door close before he went to the window to continue his surveillance of the house next door. Worry beaded a sweat on his brow. He took out his cell phone and placed the first of a series of update calls. "Yeah, Raw's through. It was a vicious go, even Aggie couldn't leave it lie. Sunny's there with the Hand. The cat's still in the bag, for now."

Chapter 10 ─────────────────────

Morning.
Earth.
Border of Ephny Ridge H.O.T. (Human-Only Territory.)

Commander Troy tried not to stare at the gruesome cadaver; but the stage was too perfectly set—the killers had accomplished their goal. He was admittedly, and properly, horrified.

As the father of two sons only a little more grown than the unmourned boy hanging without grace—one of whom was working this very scene—he couldn't help the sadness that welled up in his heart. His professional experience painted a picture of every detail of the crime with the kind of denotative clarity that would have driven him to frenzy in the old days, before all of this rampant humanity stripped the beating heart from his chest. He nearly thanked the Elders out loud as his son came over with the preliminary report in hand. He welcomed the coroner's objectivity; he intended to feed on it like a vampire, anything to be distanced from the withering emotions that were threatening his civility.

"Dad, here are the initial findings." Matthew Troy was informal with his father, waiving the professional titles of sir and doctor, even as they stood in the midst of all of their colleagues. He adjusted his kuffiya over his cropped, dark brown curls just as comfortable publicly announcing his status as swain-kind as he was letting everyone know that he was his father's filial son.

Troy read through each line of the report while Matthew gave him a verbal overview. "The victim is a male, twenty-two Human Years of age. Well fed and fully developed, with no disease or debilitations present. One-hundred percent pure Human. No tagged DNA, outside markers, or signs of genetic tampering. He was fourteen weeks gravid at the time of death. The fetus was unremarkable and normally developed for the time frame."

"Please tell me that he was already gone," Troy interrupted the very clinical assessment.

Matthew took a minute to glance over the technical locus. They were standing in mud stained a deep maroon by blood and indiscernible bits of flesh that had spun free of the body as it was being mutilated. The ADF set the law, but factions like the Human league challenged every article, every pronouncement, and every single letter of it until no one could agree on what was right or wrong.

A shade of liberal grey bathed even the most egregious crime in the impartial light of unaccountable logic. Everyone had a side that they had a right to defend, and a point that exonerated them by the fact of its existence alone. In a world that prided personal freedom above all other considerations, the jails stood full of the innocent, while perpetrators were free to offend to the content of their black hearts. And the once highly-regarded Military Police settled quietly into their role as a janitorial service;

no one bothered to wonder why. Each day that passed without the discretion of common sense, it became more self-evident that morality had been sacrificed on the altar of the new alt-liberty.

"The gunshot brought him down, but didn't kill him. By the volume of blood, the haste of the extraction and the deep, ear-to-ear cut across his throat that were all premortem wounds, it's fair to say that he lived to see the worst of what was done to him." Matthew's voice dropped with reverence. "The removal of teeth, facial tissue, and both hands was done postmortem in an crude attempt to delay identification."

"Yeeeaaahhh, that's fucked up wrong." Lieutenant Tea´ sighed. The Yomin crossbred warrior was more familiar with abject horror than she cared to admit. "I sure hope the Human's Devil is real and waitin'."

"Where are we, exactly?" Troy wondered out loud. "Between the Kama-Zhe province and Gard Bridge City?"

"Yes." The affirmation came from his partner—a tall, ebony Micromegt warrior, with a soft, sweet voice. Commander Ilaheh left the group that she'd been supervising to confer with her other half. They had all of the evidence they needed in hand. Now it was time to put the pieces together to exactly the avail that they'd come to expect—none—but at least their records would be complete. "There is a new off-worlder's settlement approximately fifty miles down the mountain, quite close to Gard Bridge City. Recall you, there is a UEDF-TAU officer, one Lieutenant Aslaug, working with us through the Unity Program. She mentioned that she lives in a settlement called Solito Lake, but it is exclusively for her people's use. The Foundation still has a manned post at the Otswald bus depot less than a mile away. That was likely where the young sir was trying to go."

"This violence has already spread as far as it was meant to." Troy took comfort from the only bit of solace the situation had to offer. "Wrap things up here. See if there's anyone available for an interview."

"Yeah, good luck with that," Lieutenant Tea´ scoffed at the far-fetched notion. It would take an absolute miracle to make the representatives from the H.O.T. admit that the victim was a Human let alone anything else. "Counselor Tommy's gonna make ya'llz nerves bad when you toss that tidbit on his to-do list."

"It is just protocol." Commander Ilaheh didn't like the flavor of their duty any more than the lieutenant did.

"Formalities are gonna be the death of us all." Lieutenant Tea´ waved as she strolled off to make the Foundation counselor's day that much harder. "Take what I'm sayin'."

"Before we start our rounds, we should check in with Counselor Kelly," Ilaheh suggested as she left the cordoned-off scene with her partner. "She is at the aforementioned bus station's Foundation office."

"If you think that we should." Troy was neither here nor there about it. He just wanted off the mountain and away from all things Human as quickly as possible.

"I spoke to her only moments ago. She said it would save us a trip to Gard Bridge City if we did stop by."

"Hoh?" His curiosity was roused as they piled into their MP cruiser.

Commander Ilaheh encouraged him to do most of the driving because she liked to use the time to go over her notes. She'd already written a veritable dissertation as she collected evidence and made her private observations of the scene. When they got back to base headquarters she'd regale him for hours with some very clever considerations and a few sobering theories that would go a long way toward writing a cohesive, plausible report.

A portion of a mile only took seconds to travel on the superpass highway. Troy wondered why he bothered to get on it at all. It actually took longer to negotiate the on-ramp and wait for an opening than it would have to have just taken the mountain's side road. Ilaheh hadn't noticed a thing; she'd been busying herself, as usual, and hadn't looked up once until a din muffled by the cruiser's sound-dampening interior forced her to seek out its source.

Troy turned into the bus depot's parking lot to find it teeming with excitement. Ilaheh's writing became frantic. She tried to describe in as much detail as she could the furor that was caused by an assemblage of protesters that clamorously declared their peaceful intentions while they tried to whip themselves into a disastrous frenzy.

"Lieutenant Tea´, we need support down at Otswald ASAP," Troy radioed as they moved towards the rumpus.

"Yes, sir," she responded.

"Backup is on the way," he told Ilaheh.

"Why did the Counselor not call for it sooner?" she questioned out loud as the crowd parted to let them through. They might have been an angry mob, but they weren't crazy enough to challenge the Military Police.

"I am the Voice of the People." A disheveled, sweaty man who looked as if he hadn't eaten in days stepped forward. "We will be heard!"

"Sir, keep order here." Four short words was all Commander Ilaheh had to offer him. She'd recognized the troublemaker by scent alone. Every time they had a run-in with the street prophet he had a savor of unwashed, animalistic desperation to go along with his fiery rhetoric.

"Order is exactly what the people demand! We demand our say!" he bellowed with much more power than one would think such a flimsy man could muster. "We will not be blamed for the crimes of extremists! We will not let the MP march into Gard Bridge City to stand us accused of crimes against humanity!" He flayed his arms putting more of his rank musk in the air than the people gathered around him could stand. A wide channel formed in time with his excited words. "Constable, there is a difference between protecting our racial identity and genocide. We will not be stained with the spilt blood of a Law Malfeasant just because we are Humans!"

The crowd cheered loudly but not as long as they might have liked to because of the arrival of the MP reinforcements and more armored troopers than the naked mob was prepared to deal with.

"I am certain that a Foundation representative with be with you very soon." Commander Ilaheh steered the now nervous Voice of the People's attention back towards her. "It would behoove one and all to keep order until then."

The two commanders entered the Foundation office that was absolutely serene in an unsettling manner. All places of doctoring had an undercurrent of dispassionate sterility that made death seem close at hand. Counselor Tomas, verenigd twin to Counselor Tommy who was still on Ephny Ridge, didn't look up from the paper work he was reviewing under the brittle scrutiny of the two regular psychologists who were stationed here to address them. He'd been in meld with his brother all day, and as far as he was concerned he'd been in contact with the constables all day, too.

Counselor Kelly lingered on the phone trying to calm her agent in the field. Tommy was indeed having his way with anyone he could get a hold of for leaving him to deal with the H.O.T.'s representatives. Finally, Kelly found the words that brought a tentative peace. They could tell by the way Tomas' shoulders had come down from around his ears that Tommy acquiesced, and they all breathing a grateful sigh of relief.

"Commander Ilaheh. Commander Troy." Ever the modernist, Kelly acknowledged each constable separately. "Such tides and times."

"Indeed," Ilaheh agreed. "Complete with heat and fury, but not for the victim."

"I was just about to called you by, you must have read my mind." Kelly brandished a report pad with a game-changing smirk. "It pricked me how *quickly* the Voice of the People had rallied his forces, complete with painted signs."

"He must have a new police scanner." Troy soughed wearily at the thought of having to search the Voice's nasty hoarder-house for more contraband technology. The last time he went in there he had to have a tetanus shot.

"Or he might know more than he should about a crime which has just come to light." Kelly passed along her suspicions.

"You believe that the victim came from Gard Bridge City." Ilaheh extrapolated from the hints Kelly had dropped.

"Only since the defense satellite census report came in for the surrounding settlements." She transmitted the data package to the constables' report pads. "Both Ephny Ridge and Solito Lake have all persons accounted for. Their communities are small and easy to track. But an open city the size of Gard Bridge, with urban and suburban residence, has a tolerance of twenty percent inaccuracy, which they greatly exploit."

"The price of freedom," Troy summed up all of their thoughts in four short words that were every bit as curt as the ones his partner had passed, unvarnished, to the people's self-appointed demagogue.

"All this to gain political advantage?" Ilaheh considered a new theory which now involved a regular family, shamed by a son's indiscretion, putting a private end to their problem. As is typically the case, tongues are not easily held. At some soon-after point the Voice of the People heard gossip of the body in the woods outside of Ephny Ridge and quickly mustered to use the tragedy to further his agenda.

It didn't change a thing. No one was likely to be punished, not because of drunken canards whispered in the middle of the night to a half-crazed town crier. There was no way to prove one single element of her supposition. Even after they detained the Voice and all of his people for questioning, she anticipated that not a usable word would come out of the lengthy rambling statements they'd be combing through for the next week straight. She watched her partner draw his own conclusion in silence. His eyebrows lifted and she could tell that he had a different take on things that he may, or may not, share.

"The Human League has been trying for Human Years to get the H.O.T. zones disbanded." Troy noted but stopped short.

"Now what to do, Counselor?" Ilaheh knew why her partner chose to keep quiet. He didn't want to open the floor up to an endless debate—which is what psychiatrists did best. As it stood, she was surprised by how directly Counselor Kelly was able to convey her suspicions without a plethora of alternative reasons.

"Make a visit of notification to Solito Lake on your way back to the valley. I am sure that they are the only ones out of the loop. Be candid but reassuring." Kelly signed off on the order. "The phone numbers for the settlement's contact person, Dr. Esperanza Ibanez, are highlighted."

"She has a cell phone?" Commander Ilaheh wondered aloud. Cell phones were level five technology and unavailable to the general public.

"Dr. Sunduvall tells me that the Solito Lake Village is a wonder unto itself, though I have not had the occasion to visit." Kelly added a bit of expose´.

"Is that fair warning, Counselor?" Troy smiled coquettishly as they turned to leave.

"Take it how you will, good sir," Kelly responded with her own glorious smile, "but be sure to tell me all about it."

United we stand STRONG. Everyone is welcomed and necessary. We will bring all of our resources to bear to defend our own. We will put freedom and peace ahead of personal gain.